S0-ABN-534

Ex-Library: Friends of
Lake County Public Library

GOLDEN BLOOD

GOLDEN BLOOD

by
Jack Williamson

illustrated by Steve Fabian
and J Allen St. John

TAMERLANE PRESS

LAKE COUNTY PUBLIC LIBRARY

3 3113 02810 8761

GOLDEN BLOOD

Text copyright © 1933, 1960
by Popular Fiction Publishing Company.
This edition copyright © 1978 by Jack Williamson.
Text illustrations copyright © 1978 by Steve Fabian.

Printed in the United States of America.
all rights reserved

A slightly different version of this novel was originally
serialized in *Weird Tales Magazine*, April-September 1933

First cloth edition — April, 1978
Published by Bill Ross and Tim Underwood

The cover painting by J. Allen St. John is from
the collection of Russell Swanson.

CONTENTS

ILLUSTRATIONS

RETROSPECT: 1977

Golden Blood *ran as a six-part serial in* Weird Tales, *beginning in the issue for April, 1933. To my immense delight, the first two installments had splendid covers by J. Allen St. John, the great Burroughs illustrator, one of them reproduced on the jacket of this edition. Farnsworth Wright, the editor, wrote me about this painting:*

"I have just seen the rough color-sketch of St. John's cover for Golden Blood, *and am enthusiastic about it — that colossal golden tiger looming gigantic in the sky, with one paw melting into the mountain ridge beneath it; and in the foreground Price and Fouad sitting astride their white camels and looking quite Lilliputian by comparison. And what a gorgeous splash of color — the golden-yellow tiger, the vivid green of Vekyra's robe and the intense crimson of Malikar's garment! Allah!*

"St. John was so fascinated with the story itself that he stayed up until one in the morning to finish reading it, after his wife went to bed. His enthusiasm for the story has encouraged me to order not one, but two covers for your story. St. John will also do all the black-and-whites. . . ."

I needed such encouragement. Turned twenty-five that April, I was back in college — taking courses in literature and science at the University of New Mexico — after a first experimental year as a full-time freelance writer. Though I suppose I had really done surprisingly well for a half-taught farm boy trapped in the depths of the great depression, the experiment had been no dazzling success.

The depression had just wiped out my two best-paying markets, Strange Tales *and the old Clayton* Astounding. *The*

Golden Blood

editors of Argosy *had rejected* Golden Blood, *tempering my disappointment only slightly with their approval of "the nice color." For all my joy in the sale to Wright and the St. John covers, the funds of* Weird Tales *were in a closed Indianapolis bank, holding up my pay for the novel.*

I had a lean spring and summer, but Wright began making monthly payments that fall, as soon as he was able. The rate was only a penny a word, but that was good money for me and probably all he could afford—I doubt that Weird Tales *ever earned much for anybody, but I still have very warm recollections of the magazine and the people who made it.*

A literary historian might explain Weird Tales, *I suppose, as one natural response to American society of the 1920s and 1930s. World War I had failed to make the world safe for democracy, national prohibition had created more criminals than saints, and business as usual had come to grief in the Wall Street crash and the great depression. Though* The Saturday Evening Post *was still printing fiction about shrewd young white males who made good in the Puritan way, such satirists as H.L. Mencken and Sinclair Lewis were exposing the hypocrisies of the dollar-worshippers who still publicly professed the traditional standards they privately ignored. Ernest Hemingway and many another embittered idealist fled the country.* Weird Tales *offered an easier and cheaper escape, the monthly fare only two bits, into fantastic worlds that made a rich contrast to its gray pulp pages.*

Weird Tales *was vastly different from* Unknown, *another great fantasy magazine that was edited by John W. Campbell in the years 1939 to 1943.* Unknown *stories were generally written with better craftsmanship and more sophistication than* Weird Tales *stories, but they were nearly all consciously tailored to fit*

*the fantasy formula Campbell had borrowed from H. G. Wells:
each story should be built on just one new premise, with everything else as familiar and logical as possible. The result was often
a sort of intellectual game, with more emphasis on paradox than
on satisfying substance; exciting at first,* Unknown *developed a
certain sameness.* Weird Tales *fiction was sometimes crudely
written, sometimes polished, but — except for the work of a few
such popular regulars as Seabury Quinn — seldom predictable. It
ranged from the "weird-scientific" — as Wright would have called*
Golden Blood — *to the farthest reaches of the supernatural and
the occult, with no taboo, he once told me, except necrophilia.
Each issue was a fresh adventure.*

*Wright himself I liked and admired. A tall quiet man, of unex-
pected dimensions. His face and his gait were already stiffened
when I first knew him with the Parkinson's paralysis that finally
killed him. His mask-like expression gave an odd incongruity to
his rich humor. Something of a literary scholar, in 1935 he published his own edition of* A Midsummer Night's Dream, *with 25
illustrations by Virgil Finlay and notes of his own, in pulp magazine format as the first volume of* Wright's Shakespeare Library.
*Sadly, there was no second volume. I have always been grateful
for the generous recognition he gave me at a time when I was
almost desperate.*

*Once, when I was in the office at 840 North Michigan
Avenue — an address I will never forget — he even offered to give
me the two St. John paintings for* Golden Blood. *I had to refuse
them at the time; a wandering freelance, I had nowhere to keep
them. By the time I had a place, they were gone. They are worth
thousands, of course, to their owners now.*

Bill Sprenger, the business manager, was a cheerful, helpful

Golden Blood

young chap, and the Weird Tales *authors I met were as various and fascinating as the magazine itself. The first was Edmond Hamilton, who became one of my closest friends. A lean, dark Pennsylvanian, just a few years older than I, he had begun his long* Weird Tales *career in 1926. He produced his sagas of the far future with energetic enthusiasm, jabbing the typewriter with two vigorous fingers and mailing off his manuscripts in first draft. Wright never rejected them. A master story-teller, Hamilton had a knowledge and love of books and literature that extended far beyond the pulps he wrote for. His craftsmanship grew steadily through the years, and he did more to create the great central myths of science fiction than the current crop of academic critics gives him credit for. His unexpected death, early this year, was a personal jolt to me.*

We first met in the summer of 1931, after discovering through Jerome Seigel that we were both fans of A. Merritt. In the course of our correspondence, I had agreed to a plan of his to drift down the Mississippi in a houseboat, in Huck Finn's wake — a project that now seems a little rash, since neither of us had ever been in a boat before. Meeting in Minneapolis, we gave up the houseboat for a skiff with an outboard motor, which took us almost to Vicksburg before the motor failed. We got passage back to Arkansas and on down the river on the Tennessee Belle, *an old stern-wheeler whose captain was straight out of Mark Twain. In New Orleans we spent a couple of weeks enjoying the company of E. Hoffman Price, an early* Weird Tales *regular, whom Hamilton had met in Chicago on his way to join me.*

Price impressed me, not only as an able pulp fictioneer but also as a real-life soldier of fortune. A native Californian, a veteran calvaryman, and a West Point graduate, he had served in

the Philippines, on the Mexican border, and in France. His hob-
bies included rare liqueurs and the dueling epee. He had limitless energy, with a vast capacity for non-stop motor trips and
night-long talk. An enthusiastic Orientalist, he was learning
Arabic, collecting Persian rugs, and spinning tales of the Peacock
Throne. When I came to write Golden Blood, the hero was
named for him.

The novel was written in the fall of 1932, on the family ranch
in eastern New Mexico. Later I built a two-room cabin there,
where I could retire in hard times to live on nothing a month
while I wrote another story, but that fall I worked in the family
living room after others were in bed, writing until dawn by a coal
oil lamp.

I had never been to Arabia, a fact that doesn't matter. I had
seen sand dunes and sandstorms enough in New Mexico, but
the story came out of a living legend of the mysterious East that
was only remotely related to hard reality. With equal relish, I had
read T.E. Lawrence's Seven Pillars of Wisdom and George
Allan England's Flying Legion. A handful of travel books had
given me notes on the language and culture of the Arabs, but the
landscape of the novel is closer to the Arabian Nights than to the
National Geographic.

In the way of the fabulous pulp fictioneers I had chosen for
models, I had been sending stories out in first draft—commonly
with better success than might have been expected—but I spent
more care than common on Golden Blood, rewriting long sec-
tions of it before I typed the finished copy. I wanted to break into
Argosy, then still a great adventure pulp, publishing the writers I
most admired and paying them five or six cents a word. To fit
the Argosy pattern, I built it into six installments, each ten thou-

Golden Blood

sand words, each ending with a serial climax. Though Argosy
sent it back, my hurt was soothed by Wright's acceptance and
St. John's enthusiasm.

St. John, by the way, suggested one change in the story. "He
says it ends too abruptly," Wright wrote me, "that the intrusion
of the airplane into the dreamland setting of the story is too sudden, and leaves him with a sense of disappointment. He thinks
the last page in the ms. should be stretched out to fill two pages."
I did rewrite the ending, and Wright found the new version "now
much more artistic."

I am deeply grateful to the publishers for this handsome new
edition. Generously, they have allowed me to revise the text,
but for the most part I have limited myself to striking out needless
commas and deleting a few purple or redundant adjectives. To
have done much more might have spoiled the story, because I
am no longer the intense young romanticist who wrote it. The
details of character and plot had nearly all escaped my memory
in the years since I had looked at it. Rereading it almost as if it
had been by some other hand, I found it unexpectedly absorb-
ing, and I was happy to recover its mood and color, which I
could hardly create now.

It belongs to the lost world of the early Weird Tales, from
which Price and I survive, along with Bob Bloch and Frank Long
and too few others. Later, of course, during the 1940s and after,
a whole firmament of new stars appeared, and after Wright's
death the magazine had another able editor, Dorothy McIlwraith,
but I was no longer writing for it by then.

At one time and another I met several others of the old guard.

Jack Williamson

Kirk Mashburn, who worked at some dull job in Houston and wrote about exotic vampires. Clark Ashton Smith, Poe-like poet and eccentric sculptor. Otis Adelbert Kline, a rival of Edgar Rice Burroughs, who ran a successful literary agency. August Derleth, an enormously energetic and prolific writer who set up Arkham House to put H.P. Lovecraft into hard covers. Lovecraft and Robert E. Howard were two great figures I never did meet, though Wright passed along Lovecraft's comment that he liked the "striking tableaus" in Golden Blood. *Those I knew were gifted writers and good companions, united in a special fellowship where I was proud to be accepted.*

Now in 1977, all that seems far away and long ago. Revived by Leo Margulies, Weird Tales *has come and gone again. The last of those who made it are vanishing too fast. The old myths of the magic Orient and mysterious Arabia have faded away, along with the last blank spaces on the map. The halls of the New Mexico University where I teach are crowded now with aggressive young Saudis and Iranians come to complete their M.A.s in business administration.*

Yet it strikes me now that Golden Blood *was prophetic in its own odd way. True, nobody has yet found the sand-drifted treasures of ancient Anz, or golden vapor rising from within the earth to transform living things. But the adventurous* farengi *with their maps and seismographs have in fact discovered incredible treasure beneath the Empty Abode, oil and gas that turn to actual gold.*

Jack Williamson

GOLDEN BLOOD

HE NOONDAY Arabian sun is curiously like moonlight. The eye-searing brilliance of it, like the moon, blots out all color, in pitiless contrast of black and white. The senses withdraw from its drenching flame; and the Arab *kaylulah* or siesta is a time of total surrender to supernal day.

Price Durand, sprawled beneath a sun-faded awning on the schooner's heat-blistered deck, lay in that curious half-sleep in which one dreams yet knows he dreams, and watches his visions like a play. And Price, the waking part of his mind, was astonished at his dream.

For he saw Anz, the lost city of the legend, where it stood hidden in the desert's heart. Mighty walls girdled its proud towers, and away from their foot stretched the green palm groves of the great oasis. He saw the gates of Anz open in the dream, massive valves of bronze. A man rode out upon a gigantic white camel, a man in gleaming mail of gold, who carried a heavy ax of yellow metal.

19

The warrior rode out of the gate, and through the tall palms of the oasis, and into the tawny dunes of the sand-desert. He was reaching for something, and his fingers kept tight upon the helve of the great ax. And the white camel was afraid.

A fly came buzzing about Price's head, and he sat up, yawning. A damned queer dream, that! He had seen the old city as vividly as if it had actually been before his eyes. His subconscious mind must have been at work on the legend: there had been nothing in the story about a man in golden armor.

Well, it was too hot to worry about a dream, too hot to think at all. He mopped the perspiration from his face, and stared around him with eyes narrowed against the blinding glare.

The Arabian Sea blazed beneath the merciless sun, a plane of molten glass. The blazing sky was tinged with copper; dry, stinging heat drove down from it. A tawny line of sand marked the northern horizon, where the desolate shifting dunes of the Rub' Al Khali met the incandescent sea. The schooner *Inez,* as furtively sinister as her swart Macanese master, lay motionless upon the hot, steely ocean, a mile offshore, her drooping, dingy sails casting narrow and comfortless shadows upon greasy decks.

Price Durand, lounging beneath his tattered awning, was saturated with the haunting loneliness of hot sea and burning sand. The brooding, shadowy hostility of the unknown desert so near flowed about him like a tangible current, silent, sinister.

His emotions had become oddly divided, he was thinking, in the long days since the schooner had left the Red
Sea, as if two forces in him were struggling for mastery.

Price Durand, the world-weary soldier of fortune, was
afraid of this cruelest and least known of the deserts of the
world, but not, of course, to the extent of wishing to aban-
don the expedition; he was not the sort to quit because he
was afraid. But he struggled against the tawny, brooding
power of the desert, fiercely determined not to be mastered
by its silent spell.

And the other, new-born part of him welcomed the
haunting spirit of the desert, surrendered to it gladly. The
very loneliness beckoned, the stark cruelty was a mute
appeal. The same stern hostility of the land that frightened
the old Price Durand was a fascinating allure for the new.

"See Fouad's coming," boomed Jacob Garth's calm
voice from the foredeck. "Kept the rendezvous to a day.
We'll be starting inland by Monday."

Price looked up at Jacob Garth. A huge, gross man, with
a deceptive appearance of softness that concealed his iron
strength. His skin looked white and smooth; it seemed
neither to burn nor tan beneath the sun that had cooked all
the others to a chocolate brown.

Holding the binoculars with which he had been scanning
the red line of the coast, Jacob Garth wheeled with ponder-
ous ease. He evinced no excitement; his pale blue eyes
were cold and emotionless. But his words woke the
schooner from sun-drenched sleep.

21

Joao de Castro, the swarthy and slant-eyed Eurasian master, scum of Macao, burst out of his cabin, shrieked excited questions in Portuguese and broken English. De Castro was small, physically insignificant, holding authority over his crew by sheer force of cutthroat hellishness. Price had no great liking for any of his strangely assorted fellow adventurers; but Joao was the only one of them he actually hated. That hatred was natural, instinctive; it had risen from some deep well of his nature at first sight of the man; and Price knew the little Macanese returned it cordially.

Jacob Garth silenced the feverish questions of the master with a single booming word: "There!"

He handed his binoculars to the little man, pointed at the line of undulating sand across the steely sea.

Price's attention went back to Garth. After three months he knew no more of the man than on the day he had met him. Jacob Garth was a perpetual enigma, a puzzle Price had failed to solve. His broad, tallow-white face was a mask. His mind seemed as deliberate and imperturbable as his massive body. Price had never seen him display any shadow of emotion.

Presumably, Garth was an Englishman. English, at any rate, he spoke, unaccented and with the vocabulary of an educated man. Price imagined that he might be a member of the aristocracy, ruined by the war, and attempting this fantastic expedition to recoup his fortune. But the supposition was unconfirmed.

It was strange, and yet almost amusing, to watch Jacob Garth standing motionless and immutable as a Buddha, while the excitement his words had created ran like a flame over the ship.

The men sprang up from where they had been lounging on the deck or came running up the companionway to line the rail in a shouting, jostling throng, oblivious of the beating sun, staring at the horizon of sand.

Price surveyed the line, speculatively. A hard lot, this score of life-toughened adventurers who called themselves the "Secret Legion." But a hard lot was just what this under-taking demanded; no place here for pampered tenderfeet.

Every man of the "Secret Legion" had served in the World War. That was essential, in view of the actual nature of the schooner's cargo, which was manifested as "agri-cultural machinery." None was younger than thirty, and few were more than forty. One, besides Price, was an American; he was Sam Sorrows, a lanky ex-farmer from Kansas. Nine were British, selected by Jacob Garth. The others represented half a dozen European countries. All were men well trained in the use of the implements in the cargo; and all were the sort to use them with desperate courage, in quest of the fabulous treasure Jacob Garth had promised.

With only their naked eyes, the men at the rail could see nothing. Reluctantly, Price got to his feet, crossed the hot deck to where Garth stood. Without a word, the big man took the binoculars from the captain's trembling hands and handed them to Price.

"Look beyond the second line of dunes, Mr. Durand."

Endless ranks of heaving red-sand crests marched across the lenses. Then Price saw the camels, a line of dark specks, creeping across the yellowish flank of a long dune, winding down towards the sea in interminable procession.

"Sure it's *your* Arabs?" he asked.

"Of course," boomed Garth. "This isn't exactly a main street, you know. And I've had dealings with Fouad before. I promised him two hundred and fifty pounds gold a day, for forty mounted warriors and two hundred extra camels. Knew I could depend on him."

But Price, having heard before of Fouad El Akmet and his renegade band of Bedouin *harami*, knew that the old sheikh could be depended upon for little save to slit as many throats as possible whenever profitable opportunity offered.

The stinging sun soon drove the men back to the narrow shadows. Stifling silence settled again, and the vast, unfriendly loneliness of the Rub' Al Khali—the Empty Abode—was flung once more over the little schooner drenching in blinding, merciless radiation.

By sunset of the next day the last box and crate had been landed from the schooner and carried up beyond reach of the waves by Fouad's forty-odd men. The neat, tarpaulin-covered piles stood beside the camp, surrounded by tents and kneeling camels.

Price, guarding the piles with an automatic at his hip, smiled at the consternation that would ensue in certain diplomatic circles if it became known that the "agricultural implements" in these crates had gone into private circulation.

Mentally, he ran over the inventory, chuckling.

Fifty new Lebel rifles, .315 caliber, five-shot, sighted to 2,400 meters, with 50,000 rounds of ammunition.

Four French Hotchkiss machine-guns, air-cooled—an important consideration in desert warfare—also .315 caliber, mounting on tripods, with 60,000 rounds of ammunition in metal strips of thirty rounds.

Two twenty-year-old Krupp mountain guns, which had seen service in several Balkan wars, with five hundred rounds of ammunition, shrapnel and high explosive.

Two Stokes trench mortars, and four hundred ten-pound shells to match.

Four dozen .45 automatics, with ammunition. Ten cases of hand grenades. Five hundred pounds of dynamite, with caps and fuses.

And looming near him, beside a stack of oil and gasoline drums, was the most ambitious weapon of all: a light-armored, three ton army tank, mounting two machine-guns, equipped with wide treads specially designed for operation over a sandy terrain.

Price had wanted to bring an airplane also. But Jacob Garth had opposed the suggestion, without any good reason save that landing and taking off would be difficult in the sand-desert. Price, for once, had deferred, without suspecting the motive of the other's opposition.

Many weeks of cautious, anxious effort, and many thousands of dollars—Price's money—had been paid for this paraphernalia of modern war, to equip the "Secret Legion."

From his place by the tarpaulin-covered crates, Price watched Jacob Garth coming away from the empty schooner.

He noticed curiously that Garth had brought all the men from her, even de Castro. As the boat neared the sand, he saw that Garth and de Castro were quarreling; or rather that the little Eurasian was screaming shrill invective at the big man, who appeared placidly unconscious of him.

Price was wondering why no watch had been left aboard, when he saw the anchored schooner quiver abruptly. A muffled detonation rolled from her across the quiet sea. Price saw debris lift slowly from the deck, and yellow smoke spurt from ports and hatches.

With a curious silent deliberation, the *Inez* listed to port, lifted her black bow into the air, and slipped down by the stern.

Then Jacob Garth's booming voice drowned the lurid protestation of the enraged captain: "We won't need the ship out in the desert. And I didn't want her tempting anybody to turn back. When we find the gold, de Castro, you'll be able to buy the *Majestic* if you want!"

2. THE YELLOW BLADE

JACOB GARTH had come to Price Durand three months before, at a bar in Port Said, his pouchy, pallid face covered with a tangle of red beard. His once-white linens were soiled, limp with sweat; the sun-helmet pushed back on his head was battered, sweat-sodden.

The man possessed a puzzling strength. In his pale-blue, deeply sunk eyes was something hard and cold, a strange glint of will and power. His great, thick hand was not soft, as Price had expected; its grasp was crushing.

"Durand, aren't you?" he had greeted Price, his deep voice richly resonant. Keenly his pale eyes appraised Price's six-feet-two of solid, red-headed body; penetratingly his cold eyes met Price's unwavering, deep-blue ones.

Price studied him in return, found something to pique his curiosity. He nodded.

"I understand you are the sort who can be called a soldier of fortune?"

"Perhaps," Price admitted. "I have cultivated a certain taste for excitement."

"I have something that should interest you."

"Yes?" Price waited.

"You have heard the desert tales of Anz? I don't mean the village of Anz in North Arabia. The Anz of the lost oasis, beyond the Jebel Harb range."

"Yes, I know the Arab legends, of Magainma and other lost cities of the central desert. New *Arabian Nights.*"

"No, Durand." Garth lowered his mellow voice. "The Bed-ouin tales of Anz, fantastic as they are, are based on truth.

Most folk-tales are. Even the *Arabian Nights* have a core of true history. But I've something more than hearsay to go on. If you will be so kind as to accompany me aboard my schooner, I'll give you the details. The *Inez*—down in the outer basin, by the breakwater."

"Why not here?" Price motioned to a table in the corner.

"There are certain articles I want to show you, by way of evidence. And—well, I don't care to be overheard."

By reputation Price knew the *Inez* and her Macanese master—and knew nothing good of either. Any enterprise in which they were involved promised dubious adventure. But in his present mood, restless, weary of the world, that was not to his distaste.

He nodded to the big man.

Joao de Castro welcomed Price aboard, with a twisted smile upon his swart face, which had been so eaten away by smallpox that it was hairless. The oblique eyes of the little Eurasian went fleetingly to Jacob Garth, and Price caught a furtive question in them. The big man pushed by him, almost roughly, led the way to a dingy cabin, amidships.

Locking the door behind them, he turned to face Price.

"It's understood you say nothing of this, unless you accept my proposition."

"Very well."

He studied Price again, nodded. "I trust you."

He made Price sit down, while he set a bottle of whisky and two glasses upon the cabin table. Price refused the drink, and Jacob Garth said abruptly:

"Suppose you tell me what you know of Anz—the lost Anz."

"Well, simply the usual story. That the inner desert used to be fertile, or at least inhabitable. That it was ruled by a great city named Anz. That the spreading deserts cut the city off from the world a thousand years or so ago.

"It's just what might be expected, considering the Arab imagination, and the fact that southern Arabia is the biggest blank spot on the map, outside the polar regions."

Jacob Garth spoke with slow emphasis:

"Durand, that legend, as you have outlined it, is true. Anz exists. It is still inhabited—or at least the old oasis is. And it is the richest city in the world. Loot for an army."

"I've heard men say such things before," Price observed. "Do you *know?*"

"You may judge the evidence. I've been exploring the fringes of the Rub' Al Khali for twelve years—ever since the war. I've lived with the Bedouins and run down a thousand legends. Most of them turned out to be simply distorted versions of the story of Anz.

"And, Durand, I've been as far as the Jebel Harb range."

That statement raised Price's estimation of the man. He knew that these mountains were considered as mythical as the lost city beyond them. If Jacob Garth had seen them, he must be far more than the unwieldy mass of flesh that he appeared.

"I had five men," he went on. "With rifles. But we couldn't pass the Jebel Harb. Durand, those mountains were guarded! I fancy the people of Anz know more about the outside world than we know about them. And they aren't anxious to resume communications.

"We had rifles. But they attacked us with weapons that, well, the details are rather unbelievable. But the five with

29

me were brave men, and I came back alone, though not altogether empty-handed. The evidence I spoke of."

Moving with a certain cat-like ease, Jacob Garth opened a locker and brought Price a roll of parchment—a long, narrow strip of cured skin, dry, cracked, the writing upon it fading with the centuries.

"A bit faint, but legible," said Garth. "Do you read Spanish?"

"After a fashion. Modern Spanish."

"This is fair Castilian."

Price took it with eager fingers, unrolled it carefully, and scanned the ancient characters.

"Mayo del Ano 1519," it was dated.

The manuscript was a brief autobiography of one Fernando Jesus de Quadra y Vargas. Born in Seville about 1480, he was forced to flee to Portugal at the age of twenty-two, as a result of circumstances that he did not detail.

Entering the maritime service of King Manoel, he was a member of the Portuguese expedition under Alfonso de Albuquerque, which seized the east coast of Arabia in 1508. There, becoming for the second time involved in difficulties that he did not describe, he deserted Albuquerque, only to be immediately captured and enslaved by the Arabs.

After some years, having escaped his captors, and not daring to return to the Portuguese settlements, he had set out upon a stolen camel to cross Arabia, in the direction of his native Spain.

"Great hardships attended me," he related, "for want of water, in a heathen land where the true God is not known, nor even the prophet of the infidel. For many weeks I drank naught save the milk of my she-camel, which fed upon the thorns of the cruel desert.

"Then I came into a region of hot sand, where the camel died for want of water and fodder. I pushed onward on foot, and by the blessing of the Virgin Mary did come into the golden land.

"I found refreshment at a city beside groves of palms. In most hellish idolatry did I find these people, who call themselves the Beni Anz. They worship beings of living gold, which haunt a mountain near the city, and dwell in a house of gold on that mountain.

"These beings, the golden folk, took me captive to the mountain, where I saw the idols, which are a tiger and a great snake that live and move, though they are of yellow gold. A man of gold, who is the priest of the snake, did question me, and then tear out my tongue, and make me a slave.

"For three years did I labor in the mountain, and by the mercy of God I slew my guard with his own sword of gold, which I have with me. Once more with a camel provided by the goodness of the Virgin, I went toward the sea, along a road that is marked with the skulls of men.

"Again thirst has pursued me, and the evil power of the golden gods. The camel is dead, and I am a cripple; so I can never leave these mountains, in which I have found a spring. In this cave I shall die, and I pray that the vengeance of God shall fall soon upon the golden land, to purge it of idolatry and evil."

Price sat staring at the dry and brittle parchment, trying to fill out in his imagination the epic of desperate adventure that its faded letters outlined. The old Spaniard must have been made of stern stuff, to do what he had done, and to dress the camel's hide and make ink and write his memoirs—driven by some obscure impulse of egotism—even after he had resigned himself to death.

Garth's deep voice broke the spell: "What do you think of it?"

"Interesting. Very. Might be a forgery, of course. Plenty of old parchment to work on."

"I found that," said Garth, "near a human skeleton in a cave in the Jebel Harb."

"That doesn't answer my objection."

Garth smiled, grimly. "Perhaps this will. *It* would not be easily forged."

He went back to the locker, and drew out the yellow blade. Wondrously it scintillated in the dim cabin; the ruby blazed hot in the serpent's mouth. A gem-set, golden *yataghan!*

"Look at this!" he boomed, in the deep voice that was so hypnotically compelling. "Gold! Pure gold! And tempered hard as steel! Look at it!"

He swung it in a hissing circle, then handed it to Price.

A weird weapon, heavy, its broad, double-curved blade razor-keen. Price thumbed it, realized that it carried an edge no ordinary gold or alloy of gold could keep. The handle was a coiled serpent of soft gold, grasping in the fanged mouth a great, burning blood ruby.

Leaning across the table, Jacob Garth looked as extraordinary as the weapon; thick-bodied, immensely broad of shoulder, skin soft and white as a child's, cold eyes glittering

32

strange and hard and eager above the tangle of curling red beard.

"Yes, it's gold," Price admitted. No denying that—or that it was harder than any gold he had ever seen. "And the ruby is genuine."

"You are satisfied?" Garth demanded.

"Satisfied that you have something unusual—the manuscript was rather fantastic in spots. But what's your proposition?"

"I'm organizing another expedition. I'm going to take a force strong enough to break through the guarded pass, and to smash whatever resistance the people of Anz may offer, beyond. A small army, if you please."

"Central Arabia has never been conquered—and a good many nations have tried it, in the last fifty centuries or so."

"It won't be easy," Garth agreed, "but the reward will be incalculable! Think of the Spaniard's house of gold! I know the desert; you do, too. We won't be tenderfeet."

"And your proposition?"

"I need say half a million to finish equipping the expedition. I understand that you are able to advance such a sum."

"Possibly. And in return?"

"You would be second in command—I am the leader, of course, and de Castro third. Half the loot will have to be divided among the men. The remainder we shall divide in twelve shares, of which five are mine, four are yours, and three de Castro's."

Gold for its own sake meant nothing to Price. His own fortune, which he had not striven to increase, approximated four million dollars. But, at thirty-one, he found himself a wanderer, weary of life, oppressed by killing ennui, driven by vague, formless longings that he did not understand. For a decade he had been an unresting, purposeless wanderer through the tropic East, seeking—what, he did not know.

The swarthy and hostile mystery of the mountain-rimmed, barren sand-desert of the Rub' Al Khali—which the nomad Bedouins themselves fear and shun—held an obscure challenge for him. He had learned Arabic; he knew something of desert life; he had seen the fringes of the unconquered desert.

The lure of treasure was nothing. The promise of action meant more. Of struggle with nature at her cruelest. Of battle—if Garth's story were indeed true—with the strange power reigning in the central desert.

The adventure appealed to him as a sporting proposition, as a daring and difficult thing, that men had not done before. The gold of which Garth talked meant no more than a trophy.

Price was suddenly eager, more interested and enthusiastic than he had been over anything in many months. Decision came to him instantly. But something about him rebelled at taking second place in anything, at taking orders from another.

"I will have to be in command," he said. "We can share equally—four and a half shares each."

Pale and hard, Jacob Garth's eyes scanned Price's face. His deep voice rang out, almost angrily:

"You heard my proposition." And he added: "You needn't fear dishonesty. You may pay out the money yourself. You know that I wouldn't risk the Rub' Al Khali unless I believed."

"I can't go," said Price, quietly, "except as the leader."

And Garth at last had surrendered. "Very well. You take command, and we share equally."

For two months the *Inez* crept stealthily between ports of eastern Europe and the Levant, while Price and Jacob Garth accumulated by the devious negotiations required in such matters, the cargo listed on the manifests as agricultural machinery, and the score of men who called themselves the "Secret Legion."

The transactions completed and the cargo aboard, she slipped through the canal and down the Red Sea, and eastward along the Arabian coast, to the spot that Jacob Garth had designated as the rendezvous with his questionable Arab allies.

3. THE ROAD OF SKULLS

THE SHEIKH Fouad el Akmet appeared painfully surprised to learn that he was expected to accompany an expedition into the forbidden heart of the Rub' Al Khali. Jacob Garth, it developed, had engaged his services upon the promise of two hundred and fifty pounds a day, and rich plunder, without specifying where the plundering was to be done.

"*Salaam aleikum!*" he cried, in the age-old formula of desert greeting, when Price Durand and Jacob Garth entered his black tent, on the night after the sinking of the *Inez.*

"*Aleikum salaam,*" Price returned, thinking at the same time that the old Bedouin's pious greeting would have little meaning if he ever found it feasible to attack his *farengi* allies.

Price and Garth seated themselves upon the worn rugs spread against camel-saddles on the sand. Fouad sat facing them, supported by a dozen of his renegade followers, squatting in a semicircle. One of the Arabs served thick, viscid, unsweetened coffee, poured from a brass pot into a single tiny cup, which passed from hand to hand.

Price sipped the coffee, delaying the opening of negotiations; Garth's bland, pale face was inscrutable. The glitter of curiosity burned stronger in Fouad's shifting eyes, and at last he could contain himself no longer.

"We ride soon?" he asked.

"Truly," Price assented. "Soon."

"Raids," the old sheikh suggested, "against the El Murra?

36

They have many camels, of the fine *Unamiya* breed." His eyes glittered. "Or perhaps we will make war even on the *farengi?*"

Jacob Garth's hand went to the leather scabbard at his belt. Slowly he drew the golden sword, held it up.

"What think you of this?" he asked in Arabic as fluent as Price's own.

Fouad el Akmet started to his feet and came forward eagerly, the gleam of the yellow blade reflected in his eyes.

"Gold?" he demanded. Then, at sight of the snake motif of the sword's handle, of the great ruby held in the serpent's fangs, he leapt back, with a muttered *"Bismillah!"*

"Yes, it is gold," Garth told him.

"The thing is accursed!" he cried. "It is of the forbidden land!"

"Then perhaps you know the road of skulls?" Garth asked, his sonorous voice slow and even. "You perhaps have heard of the treasures that lie at the end of that road, beyond the Jebel Harb?"

"No, by Allah!" the old Bedouin cried, so vehemently that Price knew he lied.

"Then I shall show you the road," Garth told him, "for we ride to plunder the land at its end."

"Allah forbid!" The sheikh was nervously twisting a finger in his sparse, rusty beard; fear was plain in his eyes.

"Every camel will be laden with gold!" Garth predicted.

"It is forbidden the faithful go beyond the Jebel Harb," the sheikh exclaimed with unwonted religious fervor, fondling the *hijab* suspended from his neck. "Beyond is a land of strange evil; Allah and his prophet are unknown there."

"Then shall we not wage a *jehad,* a holy war?" said Price, maliciously.

An agitated whisper ran along the line of squatting men. Price caught mention of *djinn* and *'ifrits.*

"What is there to fear, beyond the mountains?" he asked.

"I know not," he replied, "but men whisper strange things of the Empty Abode."

"And what are those things?" Price insisted.

"Of course I do not believe," Fouad disclaimed his superstition, half-heartedly. "But men say that beyond the Jebel Harb is a great city, that was old when the prophet came. Its people, though Arabs, are not of the faithful, but worship a golden snake, and are ruled, not by men, but by evil yellow *djinn,* in the shape of men.

"The yellow *djinn* ride upon a great tiger, to hunt down those who cross the mountains, and take their skulls to mark their evil caravan-track to the sea. And they dwell in a castle of shining gold, upon a black mountain that is called *hajar jehannum* [the rock of hell].

"Such are the desert tales. But of course I do not believe!" Fouad insisted again, when it was quite evident that he did.

"I see now," Price remarked aside to Garth, "where our old Spanish friend got the material for his fantastic diary."

"I have seen queer things in the Jebel Harb," the other returned. "Fouad's story is more truth than he imagines. Nothing supernatural, you understand. Modern science was born in this part of the world, you know, when Europe was still in the Dark Ages. My theory is that we have to deal with an isolated offshoot of the classic Arabic civilization, on a lost oasis."

Price turned back to Fouad el Akmet, who was sitting again on his rugs, staring fascinated at the golden *yataghan.*

"We talk of the evil of the Empty Abode," Price explained in Arabic. "There is nothing for our allies to fear, for we bring with us the weapons of the *farengi.* Even should there be such things beyond the accursed mountains as men say there are, we can destroy them."

"On the morrow we shall show you our weapons," Garth agreed suavely. He and Price rose from the rugs, and returned to their own tents, leaving the old sheikh muttering uncertainly, obviously torn between fear of the desert's unknown terrors and greed for its equally unknown treasures.

At sunset on the following day, when the air was comparatively cool again, Price rode upon a borrowed camel with the old Bedouin and a group of his men to the summit of a dune above the camp. Jacob Garth had remained behind, to act as director of ceremonies.

"You have rifles," Price said, indicating the muzzle-loading trade guns the Arabs carried. "But have you such rifles as these?"

He waved an arm, and the four Hotchkiss machine-guns, waiting on their tripods below, burst into staccato song, their hail of bullets lifting little clouds of sand along the beach.

"Your rifles fire swiftly," Fouad admitted. "But what do *djinn* care for rifles?"

"We have greater guns." Again Price waved.

The Stokes mortars and the two ancient mountain guns fired at once. The crashing detonations and the whine of

shell fragments, the pits torn in the loose sand, were startling, even to Price. The more cautious of Fouad's men drew
their camels back behind the dune.

"And our chariot of death!" Price shouted, signalling
again.

The tank, which the Arabs had not seen in motion, burst
into roaring life and came lumbering up the slope of the
dune, like some gray antediluvian monster, clattering,
clanging, guns hammering viciously. For a moment the
awe-struck Arabs held their ground; then, as one, they
goaded their camels into sudden flight.

"I am sorry," Jacob Garth greeted them, when they rode
sheepishly back into camp, "that you did not remain to see
our other weapons."

"The camels were frightened," replied Fouad. "We could
not control them."

"Even as the watchers in the desert will be frightened,"
said Price. "Tomorrow we take the road of skulls?"

The old sheikh hesitated, muttering. "You will pay the
gold you promised," he asked Garth, at length, "even if we
find no treasure?"

"Yes," Garth assured him.

Price was ready. He called out a command, and four
men came staggering from the camp, beneath the weight of
a great teak chest. Silently, they set it on the sand in front of
Price. Deliberately, he found the key, unlocked it, lifted the
lid to display the splendor of glittering yellow sovereigns.

Two men might have carried the chest easily enough; but
it contained five thousand pounds sterling, in gold, repre-

senting another advance from Price's pocket. He held back the lid, let the Arabs feast avid eyes.

"For each day we will pay you this great wealth." He counted two hundred and fifty coins into golden piles, and let Fouad feel them with trembling hands. "We carry the treasure with us," he added, "in the chariot of death, and pay you when we have returned to the sea."

The old sheikh haggled, insisting upon daily payment. But Price held to his terms, and that night, in the coffee-circle, Fouad surrendered.

"*Wallah, effendi.* Tomorrow we ride and may Allah have mercy!"

It was a curious procession that left the landing-place next morning before sunrise. The Sheikh Fouad El Akmet was the leader, upon his magnificent white *hejin*. A tall, sparse-bearded, hawk-nosed man was Fouad, with a predatory glitter in his dark eyes that did not belie his unsavory reputation.

The baggage-camels were strung out behind him, laden with cases still marked "spades" or "cultivators" or "farm implements."

The Arabs rode among them; lean men, mostly, as if dried and shriveled by the desert sun, with dark stern faces, thin, tight lips and piercing eyes. Like Fouad, they wore flowing white *kafiyehs*, and rough black *abbas*, of camel's hair.

The white men were mostly in the rear, all of them save Price and Jacob Garth unused to camel-riding, and sitting their rolling, jerking mounts awkwardly and with much complaint.

Bringing up the rear came the tank, motor roaring, reek of burning oil drifting from it. The camels were afraid of it—and the Arabs regarded it as a very dubious addition to the caravan. It would stiffen Fouad's uncertain loyalty, Price thought—especially since it carried gold.

They had risen before dawn, packed the complaining camels, and breakfasted hastily, the Arabs upon dates and flaps of half-raw dough, the others upon bacon and coffee and hardtack.

Price had put himself near the head of the long line of laden beasts that wound over the first lines of dunes, away from the sea, toward the heart of the great unknown, the Empty Abode, toward desperate adventure.

It was all strong wine of life—the crisp, refreshing dawn-breeze; the glory of the scarlet sunrise, enchanting the desert with purple mystery; the strong, eager stride of the fine beast he rode; the shouting of the men, even the grumbling groans of the camels.

Caravan of strange adventure! Vague, rosy visions swam before him. He saw the "golden land" of the Spaniard's manuscript, the lost city of Anz beyond the forbidden mountains. Disillusion and ennui slipped from him. He felt young and free and powerful. He knew that he was not living in vain, that splendid deeds awaited to be done.

But the brief *elan* dropped away, as the sun rose higher. The illimitable expanse of crescent hills, dull-red and yellow, wavered and trembled in the heat, unreal. The air became stifling, almost unbreathable, laden with the alkali dust that rose from the trail in choking, saffron clouds.

Perspiration wet his body and the stinging dust clung to it. He soon felt unwashed, miserable. His eyes smarted with dust, ached from the pressure of blinding light that drove down from the sun and the blazing sky, beat back from the sand, shone dazzling from all the hot horizon.

The dry air parched his throat, and he refused himself water from his canteen to wet it—three days, Jacob Garth said it would be, to the first well. The saddle chafed him. His lip bled, where sun and alkali dust had already cracked it.

Even so, the strange urge in him did not completely die. He knew the fierce joy of conquest as he reached the crest of each new dune.

They were just losing sight of the sea, over the trackless, undulating plain of sand, when old Fouad rather apprehensively pointed out to Price a tiny white object that gleamed against the dull red waste ahead.

Reluctantly the old Bedouin turned his camel toward it. As they drew near, Price saw that it was a bleached human skull, set on a tall pole planted deep in the sand. From beside it, another was in view, perhaps a mile ahead.

"Who set it here?" Price asked the sheikh.

"How do I know?" Fouad shrugged nervously. "Men say the *djinn* of the accursed land leave here the heads of men they have lured to doom. Perhaps they mark the road to Eblis."

Price rode toward the pole. His camel shied from the unfamiliar object; he dismounted and approached it on foot. The pole, some three inches in diameter, was of reddish brown wood, very hard. The skull was some ten feet above his head, but he could see bits of hair and gristle still clinging to it.

The Arab went on, and Price waited for Jacob Garth.

"Just what do you know of these skulls?" he demanded.

"There is an unbroken line of them, extending from here to a pass in the Jebel Harb, where I found the Spaniard's bones. Presumably they go on, to Anz—I wasn't able to get beyond the mountains. They must have been here four hundred years ago, for Quadra y Vargas mentions them in his manuscript."

"This skull is no four centuries old!" objected Price. "Look at it!"

"Evidently not. It must have been recently replaced."

"But who would replace it?"

"I think I told you that I believe the people of the hidden land know more of the outer world than the outer world knows of them. I suppose they wanted to keep marked the road to the sea."

"But why use the skulls of men for markers?"

"Durable and easy to see, I suppose—and cheap."

Several times that day Price rode back along the line of march, to talk with the men. Few of them knew anything of camels. They distrusted the unfamiliar beasts, and were chafed and bruised by the lurching saddles. They complained of thirst and heat and the flame of the brazen sky.

During the intensest heat of the day they stopped and let the camels kneel to rest. Toward evening they pushed on again, until it was too dark to find the guiding skulls.

46

The next day was the same, and the next.

On the morning of the fourth day they came out upon a narrow plain of gravel, a dark slash through red-sand dunes. There they found a well—a square, uncovered pit, from which they drew water with leathern buckets and ropes of camel's hair, for beasts and men. Muddy water, bitter, brackish, almost undrinkable.

It was late afternoon when the last camel had been satisfied and the last water-skin filled. Then they pushed on again, followed by the clattering tank, into another belt of loose red sand.

Two more nights they camped among the dunes. On the morning of the sixth day from the sea they came again upon hard, rolling, flinty gravel, which sloped up to a grim and rugged wall of barren mountains.

"The Jebel Harb," Jacob Garth told Price, "where I was stopped before. We'll see trouble before we pass them— and I don't know what beyond."

In the pellucid desert atmosphere the mountains looked very near. Beetling black granite ramparts, furrowed into rugged gorges and hostile, jutting salients, luridly crowned with strata of red sandstone, with pinnacles of white limestone. Bare and tortured cliff and peak were silent and ugly as bleaching bones. No green of vegetation lined the steep-walled canyons. Unbroken, the dark cruel scarp marched across the horizon, a sinister barrier to the accursed land.

The desert is deceptive. The barrier had looked very near, but as sunset approached on the following day, the caravan was still winding up the waterless gravel slopes, which were barren of even the ordinary sprinkling of dwarf acacia and stunted tamarisks.

Fouad was unmistakably apprehensive. Leaving his usual place at the head of the caravan, he rode back to join Price and Jacob Garth. Without his leadership, his men stopped, gazing with unconcealed fear at the looming granite escarpment.

"*Sidi,*" the sheikh began, unwontedly respectful again in his anxiety. "Allah forbid that we go farther! Before us are the mountains of the accursed land, that Allah gave to powers of evil. Beyond wait the *djinn,* to set our heads upon their poles."

"Nonsense," Price said. "Didn't we show you the *farengi* weapons?"

Fouad muttered in his beard, and craftily demanded that he be paid the seven days' wages due, that he might distribute the gold to encourage his timid men.

"It would only encourage them to desert," Price told him grimly. "Not one piece, until we get back to the sea!"

"There is water in the mountains," boomed Garth. "You know we must have water."

"*Bisshai,*" Fouad agreed. "The skins are dry and the camels are thirsty. But even so—"

"Let us ride on," Price cut him off.

And the old Bedouin, grumbling, at last returned to the head of the column. By sunset they had covered half the remaining distance to the lofty pass ahead, between cleft, towering masses of dark granite, capped with bands of somber red and livid white.

Jack Williamson

It was at sunset that they saw the first weird phenomenon that heralded the coming conflict with the alien power of the hidden land.

4. THE TIGER IN THE SKY

PRICE HAD URGED his weary camel to the head of the line again, to ride beside old Fouad and bolster the Bedouin's courage. Jacob Garth was back among the men. As usual, the camels were strung out in single file; it was over a mile back to the tank, which brought up the rear, clattering and banging across the flinty gravel.

But a few miles ahead the colossal rugged precipices of black granite plunged upward to red-and-white crowns of sandstone and limestone, twin towers that grimly guarded the pass.

"Ya Allah!" the Arab renegade shrieked suddenly, terror-stricken. "Be merciful!" Beneath his dark *abba* he raised a lean arm that shook with fear, and pointed above the pass.

Lifting his eyes, Price saw a strange thing in the sky, beyond the yawning gap, above dark, tumbling rocks that were incarnadined with the red glare of sunset.

Penciled rays of light were streaming upward in a vast, spreading fan, against the violet-blue of the east. Thin, pale beams of rose and saffron, flung out as if from a single radiant point hidden below the black range.

Price was startled; something about the luminescent display seemed weirdly artificial. Fighting back his momentary fear, he turned to the trembling Fouad, who had gone white as his pigmentation allowed.

"What is it?"

"The evil *djinn* of the accursed land rise beyond the hills!"

"Nonsense! Just the rays of the sun shining past a cloud, and seeming to converge in the distance. A natural phenomenon——"

Price rapidly scanned the sky for a cloud to prove his theory, but found its indigo dome, as usual, perfectly clear. He hesitated, then went on rapidly:

"A mirage, perhaps. We always see them in the morning and the evening. They are queer, sometimes. Once, in the Sind desert, hundreds of miles from the sea, I saw a steamer. Funnels and smoke and all. Even made out the boats in their davits. Simply reflection and refraction of light, in the atmosphere——"

"Bismillah wa Allahu akbar!" the old sheikh was groaning, too overcome to listen.

Price then saw that a picture was taking form above the fan of colored rays, somewhat as if projected upon the sky by a colossal magic lantern. Yet it seemed weirdly real, stereoscopic.

What he saw was madness. He knew that it should be mirage, grotesque fancy, illusion. It should have been hallucination, merely the projection of the Arabs' fears against the sky. But he knew that it was not, knew that it was, in some strange way, a reflection of actual existence.

"The tiger of the accursed land!" Fouad was screaming. "The yellow woman of the mirage, whose fatal beauty lures men across the desert to die. And the golden god, the king of evil *djinn!*"

Abruptly the old Bedouin lifted his camel-stick, shouted at his mount, turned in panic flight.

Drawing himself back from the apparition in the sky, Price drew his automatic and called to the Arab in a deadly voice:

"Stop! You aren't going to run off. I can kill you quicker than all the *'ifrits* in Arabia!"

Fouad sputtered and cursed, but he brought his white camel to a halt. His dark eyes, wide with fear, went back to the pass.

A tiger had appeared in the sky, above the spreading rays of rose and topaz. Huge as a cloud, its image was incredibly vivid and real. A sleek, powerful beast, magnified incredibly, floating above the jagged peaks. Its sides were barred with bright, rufous gold. Vast muscles bulged its massive limbs. It looked down from the sky with tawny, terrible eyes, narrowed to black slits.

A curious, box-like saddle of black wood was strapped upon the back of the uncanny beast, like a *howdah* on an elephant. In it were two persons.

One was a man, golden-bearded, yellow-skinned, clad in red robes and wearing a crimson skull-cap. His face was sullenly cruel, marked with the stamp of sinister power. Balanced on his knee was a great spiked mace, of yellow metal.

The other was a woman, green-robed, reclining in an attitude of voluptuous ease. Her skin, also, was yellow; and her long hair, flying free, was red-golden. Slim, green-cased, her body was lithely graceful, and on her face was a perilous beauty.

Her slightly oblique eyes were tawny-green, oddly like the tiger's. Their lids were darkened, as if with kohl. Her lips were crimsoned, her golden cheeks touched with rouge, her slender fingers henna-reddened. Hers was a loveliness exotic and sinister.

Fouad's furtive movement called back Price's eyes. He saw that the whole caravan had stopped. Even the tank's clatter had ceased. He sensed the fear that ran electric along the line, from man to awestruck man, fear that might readily become disastrous panic.

The old sheikh had been edging his camel away.

"Keep still," Price warned him, "or I'll kill you!"

He was certain that the danger was not immediate, and he knew the Arabs would not desert without their leader.

His eyes went back to the picture in the sky, silent and awful in its magnitude, infinitely appalling for its eldritch strangeness. The yellow man's crafty eyes scanned the caravan. And the woman was smiling down, Price saw, at *him.*

No kind smile was it. Mysterious, enigmatic, mocking. Its evasive challenge raised in Price a vague and nameless anger; yet somehow the exotic golden beauty stirred faint awakenings of desire.

The oval, aureate face was lovely, alluring, yet subtly malicious. The greenish, tawny eyes hinted of hot passion, of burning desire and withering hate, of caprice unchecked by fear or law. They were wise with an ancient knowledge not all of good. They were bold with power unlimited and carelessly held. They watched Price, speculatively, tauntingly. . . .

The yellow-beard moved. In both great hands he raised the spiked golden mace, flourished it over the pass, in a

53

gesture definitely hostile, menacing. On his harsh face was warning . . . and *hate.*

The woman smiled down at Price, with a challenge in her tawny eyes, and ran slim, reddened fingers through the golden masses of her hair.

"See, *Howeja!*" Fouad hissed. "He warns us to go back!"

Price did not answer. His gaze was still upward, meeting the woman's enigmatic orbs, giving challenge for challenge. His own eyes were hard. Abruptly, to the old Arab's manifest surprise, he laughed, laughed long and harshly, jeeringly, at the woman, and turned away.

"A modern Lilith, eh?" he muttered. "Well, strut your stuff. We can play the game."

Then, slowly as the picture had appeared, it faded, dissolved in the darkening amethystine sky, vanished. The fan of narrow rays died beyond the pass.

The black ramparts of the Jebel Harb loomed hostile against the dusk.

Price sat on his camel, his automatic still covering Fouad El Akmet—and wondered.

The weird beings of the accursed land, then, were not all fiction. People lived beyond the mountains, people whose skins were the color of gold—not the yellow-brown of the Mongolian, but *golden;* people who had domesticated the tiger, and who must command strange powers of science.

The apparition, he was sure, had been some sort of mirage. He recalled the Fata Morgana, that he had seen once at the Strait of Messina, remembered accounts of that uncanny light-phenomenon of the German mountains, known as the Specter of the Brocken, in which colossal shadows are cast upon the clouds. But had this lost race mastered the laws of the mirage? Did they rule illusion?

If this fantastic madness had already greeted them, what would they encounter beyond the range?

5. THE SIGN OF THE SNAKE

"CONSIDER THIS ALSO," Price said: "if any man turns back, we shall pursue him with the chariot of death, and leave his skull to make a nest for scorpions."

Fouad El Akmet muttered, and twisted his finger in his scrawny beard. The Arabs had refused to go farther, on the night before, had protested, even, at camping on the spot. Now, on the following morning, the old sheikh was vainly opposing any further advance.

"*Sidi,* you know that the shadow was a warning. We may yet save our lives from the golden king of *djinn*——"

"If we go on and conquer him!"

"There is water in the pass," Garth said. "A clear, sweet well. And you know the bitter waters of the last well are many days behind. Few of you would live to taste them."

Fouad wavered visibly.

"Remember the chariot of death," Price urged. "And the gold in it already yours, if you but stay."

"*Wallah!*" the Bedouin cried at last, though with obviously tepid enthusiasm. "We ride into the pass."

The rugged masses of the Jebel Harb loomed ragged and black against a pallid glow in the east, as the caravan toiled wearily upward again, over rolling foothills that were darkly purple in the dawn.

The long line of camels wound into the pass, between soaring walls of elemental granite. The patch of sky ahead became a high curtain of scarlet flame; the desert behind was pastel of saffron and lavender.

Price rode in the lead, beside Fouad, to keep alive the uncertain spark of the old man's courage. Garth was back among the men; the tank, as usual, at the rear.

The lower pass was a gargantuan gash through living rock. Its beetling walls, marching in rough parallel, seemed almost to close above its boulder-strewn floor. As Price and the old Arab picked a cautious way upward for the tender-footed camels, the sun rose to touch the high cliffs with scarlet fire, but the canyon remained shadow-filled.

Scanning the narrowing walls ahead, Price saw a glittering flash at the base of a sandstone column, a mile up the gorge. Instinctively he goaded his camel into cover behind a gigantic fallen mass of granite.

"The pass is guarded," he called out to Fouad. "I saw the gleam of a blade, ahead. Better have your men take cover."

The Arab groaned.

Price saw the old sheikh, struck motionless with terror, staring at the man who had been riding just behind him.

That man was the Arab Mustafa, a young warrior, mounting a black she-camel of whose gait and endurance he was inordinately proud. From the shelter of the fallen megalith, Price saw Mustafa freeze suddenly into strange immobility.

The young Arab and his black camel became utterly motionless. The camel was poised rigid, in the very act of stepping, one forefoot lifted. The man leaned forward, mute wonder on his thin face, one hand lifted as if to shade his eyes. His brown *abba* and flowing white *kafiyeh* had become stiff as cast metal.

"*Ya*, Mustafa!" old Fouad howled, in terror.

A strange, swift change came over the motionless figure. Glittering tracery of white was drawn over man and camel. In seconds, a frosty film covered both. The mounted man had become a statue in white, bright with an icy sparkle.

Staring in dazed and unbelieving wonder, Price heard abrupt, crackling sounds from the figure. A breath of air cold as an arctic blizzard struck his face, chilled the sweat on his forehead.

Then he knew! Not, of course, how it had been done. But he knew that *Mustafa had been frozen to death!* By some strange agency, the temperature of his body had been suddenly lowered to a point far below zero. It was so cold that frost condensed upon it from the air.

For a moment Price was dazed by the discovery, with all that it implied of the perils ahead. Then a mind and body trained to meet unexpected emergencies responded smoothly, almost automatically.

"Quick," he called to the men behind. "Get over by the cliff, out of sight." He gestured.

A score of the Bedouins and a few of the whites had been close enough to see the tragedy. As Price's words broke their spell of terror, they wheeled with one accord in panic flight, goading weary camels to a run. In vain he shouted at them to halt, as they vanished down the canyon.

Dismounting swiftly, he slipped to the edge of the sheltering boulder and cautiously surveyed the gorge ahead. He saw nothing moving; ominous silence hung expectant between the frowning walls. He studied the base of the sandstone monolith, where he had seen that fleeting, betraying gleam that had saved him from Mustafa's fate, and quickly estimated the range.

Then, hastening back, he found the whole caravan gathered in confusion about the tank, where Jacob Garth had succeeded in stopping the fleeing Arabs. The frightened clamor ceased as he rode up.

"Refrigeration to the nth degree," he explained tersely. "The man was frozen—instantly. The white is frost. I saw the glitter of the thing that did it, up the canyon."

The pale, fat face, the cold, deep-set eyes of Jacob Garth revealed neither wonder nor fear.

"They saw us, last night," he boomed. "In that—mirage. They are ready—as they were before."

"We'll give them a run for the money," announced Price. He turned to the men and began shouting brisk orders.

"Muller, take your crews and mount the Krupps for action. Bear on the base of that sandstone cliff." He pointed. "Range is about four thousand yards."

"Yes, sir!" The little Teuton, who had been a captain of artillery in the Austrian army, saluted briskly and ran toward the baggage-camels that carried the mountain guns.

Rapidly Price gave commands to have the machine-guns unpacked and set up, to cover the ancient cannon. He had rifles and automatics served out, stationed snipers to pick off any of the unseen enemy that might appear.

When the weapons were unpacked, he sent the camels back to the rear, with Arab herdsmen. The camels were to be guarded at all costs, for their loss would mean ruin.

Jacob Garth watched silently as Price rapped out his

orders, the bland white face showing neither satisfaction nor disapproval.

"Watch Fouad," Price told him. "If he runs out on us, with the camels, we're ditched. I'm going up in the tank, where I can watch the results of our fire and signal corrections."

As the little mountain guns delivered their first bracketing shots, Price delivered final instructions, sprang upon the iron deck of the tank and climbed down through the manhole to the gunner's seat. He spoke swiftly to Sam Sorrows, who had been driving the machine, and it lurched into roaring motion.

Up the defile it lumbered, past the clustered, frightened Arabs, still mounted, under Jacob Garth's guard, past the thudding little mountain guns, past the Hotchkiss guns and snipers that protected them.

Below the fallen megalith, beside which Mustafa stood white in statuesque rigidity, Price left the tank, crept forward again to scan the upper gorge. No enemy was in view. He watched the yellow bursts of dust and smoke about the base of the sandstone column as the shells exploded, called corrections out to Sam Sorrows, at the tank, who wigwagged them back to the gun crews.

A score of shells whined over: still the enemy did not appear.

Price slipped back to the tank.

"Signal them to stop firing," he said. "Probably just wasting ammunition. And let's go ahead, to where we can see, anyhow. Do you mind?"

"You're the captain."

"It will be risky. I don't know what we'll find. Our guns may have scared them off; they may be waiting. The thing that hit Mustafa——."

Sam Sorrows was clambering back into the tank.

"Risks are up my street, or I'd be back in Kansas," he said. "Let's go!"

Price climbed in after him smiling. Here was a man! Price, himself, never tried too hard to avoid danger; he had a fatalistic faith in the Durand luck. His philosophy was simple: play the game; leave the dealing of the cards to fate, to *kismet,* as the Arabs said. And he rejoiced to find another of the same hard stamp.

Lurching, clanging, treads ringing upon bare rock, the tank roared upward between narrowing granite walls, on to the sandstone pillar. And chill fingers of fear snatched at Price's heart: the shells had fallen short!

Bright metal glittered a full hundred yards beyond the group of ragged, shell-torn craters, a fantastic device of glistening brass, of shimmering crystal, surmounted with a huge, ellipsoid mirror, scintillant with a silvery fulgor.

A single man in blue bent behind the machine.

This uncanny mechanism, Price knew, was what had killed Mustafa. Would the tank's light armor be sufficient protection against the terrific cold that had frozen the Arab rigid in a split second? He though not.

Fear numbed him, the deadliest he had ever known. Icy feet raced up his spine. Chill sweat beaded his face. Grim, tense, he bent to the machine-gun.

The harsh stutter of it rose above the song of the racing engine. But, tossing from side to side in the lurching, rocking tank, he could not aim. Splinters of rock danced about the strange glittering machine, but the old, blue-robed man behind it seemed invulnerable.

Violet light gleamed suddenly on the ellipsoid mirror. And the air in the tank was deathly cold. Price's breath crackled, as he expelled it in an involuntary gasp of terror.

With numbed hands, he kept the gun hammering. At last a stream of bullets swept the bright machine. A vivid flare of purple light enveloped it, an explosive burst of flame that left but a twisted wreck of bent metal and broken crystal. Flung back by the blast, the blue-robe fell, lay motionless.

The man was still alive when they left the tank and went to him, though burned by the explosion and riddled with bullets. He lay in his gory robe, and stared up at Price with a red grin of hate.

He had been tall. His features were of the familiar Arab type. He might have been some ensanguined, dying Bedouin.

Price bent beside him. His black eyes filmed with hate, and he whispered, in the strangely inflected Arabic of an unfamiliar dialect:

"I die. But on you, intruder, is the curse of the golden folk. By Vekyra, and by the tiger and the snake, and by Malikar the master—you shall follow me!"

He coughed blood, and died with a leer of bloody horror on his face.

Only when his final struggles had ceased did Price find the brand on his forehead, that had been hidden by the hood of his burnoose-like blue robe. Printed in gold on the dark skin was the figure of a coiled snake. It seemed burned into the skin, indelible.

Price studied it with wonder strangely akin to horror. What did it mean? Was the dead man a branded member of some grim snake-cult?

"Let's go on through the pass," Sam Sorrows proposed suddenly.

"A good idea. Might be more of them."

They clambered back in the tank, which was now silvery with its bright armor of frost where the ray of deadly cold had touched it. The defile narrowed before them, then broadened, and they lumbered across a high sandstone plateau.

They looked beyond the range.

Price had half hoped to see a fertile, inhabited oasis, but the endless plain that stretched away beyond the Jebel Harb, shimmering in a smoky haze of heat, was grim and lifeless desolation.

Long drear dunes of red sand, like stilled seas of death. Dark gravel-barrens. Lurid streaks of yellow clay. Salt-pans, glaring leprous white. Low and age-worn hills of livid lime-stone and black basalt; grim, denuded skeletons of ancient ranges.

The accursed land, indeed! All its swart vastness showed no hint of life. Nothing moved upon it save the ceaseless, silent flicker of heat, like waves of ghost-seas. Or perhaps, when the winds blew, red and ancient sands, whispering secrets of the immemorial past.

Across those wastes of desolation led the road of skulls. With his binoculars, Price could trace the white gleams of the grisly landmarks for many miles, far out into the dead solitude of the forbidden land.

What would they find at the end of the road? That is, he thought, if they lived to reach it! The perils of alien science— the encounter in the pass had assured him of that. The peril that had been promised in the yellow man's flourish of the great mace, in the mirage about the mountains. And the peril Price had read in the taunting, tawny-greenish eyes of the golden woman.

Jacob Garth met them, alone and on foot, as the tank lumbered back down the gorge. Icy apprehension had dawned in Price's heart before they heard him speak. The pale eyes in his fat, bland face were coldly unreadable as ever; his deep, suave voice carried neither concern nor self-reproach, when he said:

"Durand, Fouad got away."

Throat suddenly dry, Price managed to whisper, "The camels?"

"Gone. We're stranded. As the Spaniard was."

Price's despair gave way to a flame of useless anger.

"I told you to watch! How——"

"We were watching the tank. When it turned white, and stopped, the Arabs wheeled and dashed off, before we could stop them. Drove off the baggage-camels too. We're on foot."

Scathing criticism was on Price's tongue, but he checked it. It would do no good. Nothing, now, would do any good. Only a hopeless battle remained; battle, not with man but with the world's cruelest desert.

6. THE WHITE DROMEDARY

HE BLACK GRANITE massif of the Jebel Harb was six days behind. Still the order of march was the same: old sheik Fouad el Akmet upon his *hejin,* leading the caravan along the road of skulls; the endless line of weary camels behind, carrying the Bedouin renegades, the whites of the "Secret Legion," the paraphernalia of modern war; the tank roaring and clanging in the rear.

Two days they had rested at the well in the mountains; the white men, during the first bitter night, alone, unmounted, helpless. But dawn had brought the fugitive Arabs back from their panic-stricken flight, slipping up cautiously to see how the battle had gone. Their situation was nearly as desperate as that of the others, for both camels and men were suffering for water, obviously unable to cover the distance back to the last alkaline well. Convinced, to his own amazement, that the whites had been victorious over the evil *djinn* of the accursed land, old Fouad had been glad to rejoin the expedition.

Twice since they left the range the trail of skulls had led them to brackish, bitter pools. But no living thing had they seen, in this domain of death within the mountain barrier.

The fleet gazelles, the hyenas and prowling jackals of the desert's fringes had long been left behind. In this lifeless land, even the tamarisks and acacia and sere camel-grass were lacking. The ubiquitous desert insects, ants, spiders, scorpions, were rare. The *rakham,* the black-winged vultures that had followed ominously from the mountains, had long since deserted.

It was late afternoon, and the long caravan was winding across one of the ever more frequent red-sand strips, into the selected camping-place for the night, when Price saw the white dromedary.

A magnificent, pure-white animal, resembling the *Unamiya* camels which the El Murra breed in the borders of the Rub' Al Khali, it stood upon a bare red dune two miles off the track. Its rider, a slim, white-clad figure, appeared to be watching the caravan.

Price fumbled quickly for his binoculars, but he had hardly focussed them when the unknown rider vanished silently beyond the red dune.

At the moment Price, as the expedition's leader, was busy with the old sheikh, settling one of the difficulties that had risen as a result of the Arab's thievish dispositions and the frayed nerves of the whites. Mawson, a little Cockney machine-gunner, had attacked the Arab Hamed with his fists, accusing him of stealing a gold watch and other trinkets from his pockets, while he slept. Hamed, unable to deny possession of the articles in question, swore that he had found them on the ground, after camp was broken that morning, producing perjured witnesses to substantiate his story.

A routine affair, but one that required diplomatic settling to maintain the harmonious discipline of the expedition. The tents were already up, on a sand-rimmed plane of shale, before the case was finally adjusted, Mawson's valuables being returned, and Hamed dismissed with a warning.

Only then did Jacob Garth inform Price that he had sent three Arabs in pursuit of the lone rider they had seen.

"Don't want our arrival broadcast," the big man said. "Promised the men they could divide the spoil."

The three Bedouins had already returned with the white dromedary, which was a priceless animal, and its rider. The captive was woman.

"She's something of a beauty," Garth added. "Don't blame de Castro for wanting her."

"What have they done with her?" asked Price.

"The three divided their loot into three shares, and distributed them by lot. Kanja won the girl. He felt rather cheated, because Nur got the camel. Alie's share was her outfit: saddle and her clothing and a long golden knife—a sort of straight *jambiyah*.

"Kanja wasn't especially pleased with his share of the spoil. But de Castro saw the woman, while they were dividing up. It seems she struck his fancy; he gave Kanja his binoculars for her. Must have been hit hard—you know how he prized those glasses."

"Where is she now?"

"Joao has her tied in his tent."

"Look here!" cried Price. "We can't tolerate anything like that!"

It was Price's nature to sympathize with the under-dog, with any one mistreated or imposed upon or oppressed merely because some one else was stronger. Jacob Garth's account of the bound girl roused a dull anger in him.

"We're a long way," Garth observed placidly, "from the

67

white man's law." The pale eyes, the broad, suave, white face, held no feeling.

"But we're still white men!" Price insisted, hotly. Then, realizing that the other was unimpressed, he sought for arguments. "And even with honor and decency aside, it's an unwise way to treat the first citizen of this country that we meet."

"She can't be a very important citizen," Garth opposed, "or she wouldn't be out here alone, half dead for a drink."

"Anyhow, if we treated her fairly, she might be able to give us valuable information."

"She's going to," the huge man said calmly. "Just now she's in a huff, and doesn't want to talk. But Joao de Castro is an artist at coaxing reluctant tongues."

"You don't mean he'd torture a woman!"

"You don't know him."

Price said decisively, "I'm going to see her."

"Better leave her alone," Garth advised, in the same expressionless voice. "Joao will be irritated if you interrupt his amusement. We can't afford any trouble."

Without answering, Price strode away toward de Castro's tent, a small flame of anger in his heart.

A little group of men, whites and Arabs, were gathered in front of the tent. The captured white camel was tied down, near by. Ali was proudly displaying his share of the loot—*abba* of soft white wool, *kamis* and *cherchis* of fine-woven silk, and a thin, golden dagger, whose temper, he was declaring excitedly, was good as any steel. Nur, with gestures and elaborate pantomime, was telling the story of the chase, of the fierceness with which the girl had fought, baring his side to show a skin wound he had received from the yellow dagger.

Kanja stood aside, delightedly fondling the newly won binoculars, grinning with childish pleasure as he peered through them, first from one end of the tubes and then the other.

Price strode through the group to where the Eurasian stood at the lifted flap of the tent, his pock-marked face aglow with lust. Beside him was his henchman, Pasic, a Montenegrin, who had been mate of the *Inez*. Hairy, powerful as a bull, he deserved his usual appellation, "Black Ape."

"I'd like," Price said, "to see your prisoner, de Castro."

"D' bitch, she ess mine," the little Macanese muttered.

A moment he stood in front of Price, but his shifty oblique eyes fell before Price's stern blue ones. He stepped aside.

The girl lay upon the rough shale beneath the tent. Most of the clothing had been stripped from her—being part of Ali's loot—and her wrists and slender ankles were trussed with rough halter-ropes of camel's hair. Price had known she must be attractive, to tempt the Eurasian to part with his binoculars. But her loveliness astonished him.

Young, she was; no more, he guessed, than nineteen. The skin of her fresh, smooth body was whiter than his own. Even the oval face was not deeply tanned; she must, he thought, have worn a veil.

Bound as the girl was, she could not rise. But as Price peered into the tent she twisted into a half-upright position and glared at him in regal rage. Framed in disordered brown hair, her face was delicately strong, red-lipped. Dark her eyes were, violet-blue, and quite devoid of fear.

Without stopping to analyze his emotions—which was a thing he seldom did—Price knew at once that he could not leave her in the hands of the Macanese. And he realized at the same time that Joao would make trouble, rather than lose her.

He started impulsively into the tent, to loosen her ropes. She flung her half-bare body at him, grazed his hand with strong, flashing teeth.

De Castro seized his arm, jerked him from the tent before he could resist. Dark, slanted eyes were snapping with jealous passion.

"She ess mine!" he hissed. "Damn you, keep 'way!"

"De Castro," Price said, "I want you to turn her loose."

The thin yellow hands of the Eurasian trembled.

"Turn 'er loose?" he screamed. "Turn 'er loose, when I geeve for 'er my ver' fine binoc'lar? D' hell!"

"That's all right. I'll pay you for the glasses. Or even give you mine, if you want."

"I want 'er, not d' dam' binoc'lar!"

"I'll give you five hundred dollars——"

"D' hell! What ess money, 'ere?"

"Listen, de Castro," Price said, a new note of authority in his voice. He realized that mild measures had been a mistake. "I'm head of this expedition. I order you to untie that girl."

"*Dios!*" the Eurasian screamed, shaking in a fit of passion.

"Then I'll do it, for you."

Price started into the tent again. De Castro's yellow hand darted into his shirt front. A thin knife flashed up and down.

But Price, knowing well the familiarity of Joao's kind with knives, was alert. He evaded the slashing blade, drove a heavy fist into the pock-marked face. Savage joy filled him at the dull crunch of teeth beneath the blow.

With a bull-like bellow, the Montenegrin charged to the aid of his crony. Leaping upon the unprepared Price, he wound his long, ape-like arms around him, pinioning his arms in a savage embrace, driving his knees up in vicious blows at the loins.

Twisting furiously, but helpless in the arms of the "Black Ape," Price butted uselessly at his flat, hairy face. The Arabs gathered in a ring, applauding enthusiastically.

Pasic threw back his shoulders, dragging Price clear of the ground, helpless and gasping in the embrace that was forcing the breath from his body. The Montenegrin hitched him up, dextrously changing his hold, and Price knew that the man was about to throw him over his head, probably to fall with a broken back.

Desperately he struggled for a leg-hold, failed, kicked vainly at Pasic's legs. Then an abrupt, savage lunge tore his left arm free from that crushing grasp. Instantly he drove his elbow, with a short, jabbing blow, into the Montenegrin's solar plexus.

The man gasped; the constricting embrace relaxed for an instant. Price tore himself free of the terrible arms, darted away to hitting distance.

The "Black Ape," better provided with strength and savagery than with science, charged again, long arms flinging.

71

A quick one-two to the brutish body stopped him, a dazed expression on his flat face. Another blow, to the jaw, deliberately timed and with all Price's hundred and eighty-two pounds behind it, and the man's knees weakened. He sprawled heavily beside the groaning Eurasian.

Price went into the tent.

7. AYSA OF THE GOLDEN LAND

THE BOUND GIRL glared at him, angry hate in her violet eyes. She did not recoil from his hands; she revealed no fear—only hot wrath. White teeth flashed at his hands again. He disregarded them, busied himself with the tightly drawn knots in the halter-ropes that held her.

Suddenly she was quiet; the rage in her eyes changed to silent wonder.

The ropes loosened, he chafed her wrists and ankles to restore circulation; then slipped an arm beneath her shoulders and lifted her to her feet from the rough shale upon which she had been thrown.

She stood watching him, curious speculation in her eyes.

"Aiee, Ali!" Price called, from the doorway of the tent.

The Arab approached, the garments that had been taken from the girl still in his arms.

"Give me this woman's clothing," demanded Price.

The Arab began whining protests. Price repeated the order in sterner tones, and the Arab reluctantly surrendered the garments. He kept the golden dagger thrust in his belt, and hung avidly near.

"Now go!" Price told him shortly.

He turned and proffered the clothing to the girl. Violet eyes wide in mute astonishment, she accepted them mechanically. He looked down at her white, fresh body. With a little cry, she began slipping into the garments, swiftly and without self-consciousness.

Price watched her until she had dressed, listening to the

groans of de Castro and Pasic outside the tent, and the excited clamor of the gathering crowd. Knowing the Macanese would raise trouble as soon as he recovered consciousness, Price was anxious to get the girl away from his vicinity.

When she was ready, he took her hand, led her from the tent. After a questioning look at him, she followed willingly. Outside, however, at sight of her recent persecutors, her rage flared up again. Jerking away from him, she darted upon Ali, and snatched the golden dagger from his belt. In a moment she was above Joao, who was groaning and struggling to sit up.

"Bismillah! Laan'abuk!" cursed Ali, leaping after her to recover the dagger, which had struck his fancy because of the phenomenal hardness of its yellow metal. Seizing her arm, as she raised the blade above the Macanese, he twisted it back, painfully.

A suppressed cry of agony broke from the girl's lips; her face went white. She dropped the weapon, just as Price's fist crushed against Ali's jaw.

The Bedouin staggered away, spitting blood. The girl was biting her lip; the twisted arm hung limp. But, with the other hand, she snatched for the golden dagger.

De Castro's yellow claw was ahead of her.

Price put his foot on Joao's wrist, bent and wrenched the weapon from his hand. Seizing the girl firmly by the shoulder, he led her unresisting away, toward his own tent.

Several of the watching men started to follow. He turned, ordered them curtly back. They gathered sympathetically around Joao. Though Price had won the girl's release, he

realized the victory was only for the moment; her position was still precarious.

As usual, the tank had been stopped near Price's tent. Sam Sorrows was watching from beside it.

"Trouble in the camp, Sam," Price told him briefly.

"Over the woman?"

Price nodded.

"Thought so. Damn' queer place, this, for a woman. But I reckon one could make trouble anywhere."

"It isn't her fault."

"It never is."

"Sam, I'd like you to get back in the machine and stand guard with the machineguns for a while. There's mutiny afoot."

"Okay, Mr. Durand." The lanky man grinned, as if the likelihood of fighting were enjoyable, and climbed into the tank.

Price led the girl to his tent, indicated that she might enter. A moment she studied his face, with wondering eyes. Then she smiled, and slipped inside.

For a little time Price studied the disorganized confusion of the camp about him, on the little plain among red sand-dunes. He was near the center of the camp. Tents, piles of dunnage, saddles, kneeling camels, were scattered all around him. the crowd of men about de Castro was still increasing. Price's heart sank as he realized the inevitability of conflict. Of all the seventy men about him, Sam Sorrows was the only one he trusted.

Picking up a canteen, Price entered the tent. The girl was waiting, tense, white-faced, just within. He unscrewed the top of the canteen, shook it so that the water sloshed audibly, and held it out to the girl. Eagerly she put her lips to it, drank until Price, fearing she would make herself sick with too much water, took it away.

She laughed at him questioningly; he grinned.

Then it happened: her tortured nerves gave way. She broke suddenly into a storm of weeping. Understanding that it was only the natural reaction to her relief, and yet uncertain what to do, he went toward her, touched her shoulder, pityingly.

Shaken with uncontrollable sobs, she buried her face trustfully against his shoulder. Her brown hair, fragrantly soft, brushed against his face. Then she was in his arms.

The tempest of weeping ceased as abruptly as it had begun. The girl slipped away from Price, composed again, drying her eyes upon the corner of her *cherchis*. Seeing that she looked exhausted, Price spread a blanket on the tent-floor and invited her, with a gesture, to sit down; which she did, with a grateful glance.

"Do you speak Arabic?" Price asked her, kindly.

A moment she hesitated; then understanding dawned in her eyes.

"Yes! That is the tongue of my people, though you speak it oddly."

Her Arabic was clearly comprehensible, though it had a curious inflection. It was more nearly akin, plainly, to the classic language than to any modern dialect that Price knew. But its forms were older, even than the classic. The girl spoke the Arabic of many centuries ago!

"You are welcome," Price told her. "I am truly sorry you were treated so. I hope to make amends."

"Birkum," she replied, with so close an approximation to the modern accent that Price followed without difficulty. "I am very grateful for your rescue."

It was on his lips to tell her that the rescue was still far from complete. But it would be unkind, he thought, to worry her needlessly with the true gravity of the situation. He smiled, then asked:

"Your people are near?"

She pointed northward. "That way lies El Yerim. It is three days by camel."

"Don't worry about it," he urged. "I'll see that you get safely back."

Her eyes darkened with fear. "But I can not go back," she cried. "They would give me up to the golden folk."

"You are in trouble, besides this?" She nodded.

Price invited: "Tell me about it."

"You are strangers. You know not the golden folk?"

"No. We come from a far land."

"Well," she explained, "the golden folk are beings of gold that dwell in a mountain near El Yerim. Malikar, who is a man of gold—or a god. Vekyra, who is his—well, wife. The golden tiger, upon which they ride to hunt. And the yellow snake, which is the ancient god, and the greatest of the four."

"I see. Go on."

"Every harvest season, Malikar comes down to El Yerim upon the tiger, to select the grain and the dates, the young camels, and the slaves, that shall be sent as offering to the snake-god.

"Five days ago he came. All the people of El Yerim were gathered by Yarmud, the king. And Malikar rode among them on the tiger, choosing those he would take for slaves. He saw me, and commanded that I be sent with the camels and the grain, on the next day.

"That night my house was guarded. Though the priests say it is an honor to be offered to the snake, few take it so." The girl smiled wearily. "I tricked the guards, and slipped out into the night. In the fields I found the camel that was my father's, and rode away into the desert.

"Four days I have ridden. And I was able to bring little water or food."

Price squatted on his heels, lighting a cigarette—which operation she watched with evident astonishment—as he digested her words. Her story excited his curiosity immensely; but he felt that it would be unkind to question her at much length, dead-tired as she obviously was. But one thing he must ask:

"This tiger, and the golden people—are they really gold? Living metal?"

"I know not. It is strange that metal should have life. But they are the color of gold. They are stronger than men. They do not die—they have lived since Anz was great."

"Anz?" Price caught eagerly at the name of the lost city of the legends. Was Anz, after all, no myth, but sober fact?

"Anz," the girl explained, "was the great city where once my people lived; they still call themselves the Beni Anz. Long ago the rains came every year, and all this land was green. But a thousand years ago the desert conquered Anz, and the sands rolled over it, and my people came to the oasis at El Yerim."

And the girl added, "I was searching for Anz."

80

"Why, if it is deserted?"

She hesitated, reluctantly. Her weary eyes studied him.

"No matter——" Price began, and her words rushed swiftly:

"You may think me foolish—but there is a prophecy. The last great king of Anz was Iru. A brave warrior he was, and a just man. Tall, like you." The violet eyes dwelt upon Price. "And his eyes were blue, like yours, and his hair red. The legend speaks of those matters, for most of my people are dark," she explained.

"And the prophecy?" Price asked.

"Perhaps it is an idle tale." Again she paused, then continued with a rush: "But according to the legend, Iru is not dead. He still sleeps in the halls of his palace, in the lost city. He waits for some one to come and wake him. Then he will come out again with his great ax, and slay the golden folk, and free the Beni Anz."

"Do you believe the legend?" asked Price, smiling.

"No. It might be true. By the legend, you see, it is a woman of my name who should go to wake the king." And she added: "When I had fled from El Yerim, I had nowhere else to go."

The girl caught herself nodding, jerked back upright, smiling wanly at Price.

"One thing more, and you may sleep," he said. "What is your name?"

"Aysa," she whispered. "And I shall call you——"

"Price Durand." And he murmured softly, "Aysa. Aysa of the golden land."

She smiled, and was suddenly asleep, sitting half upright.

Price rose and laid her softly upon his blankets, in a comfortable position. She did not wake when he moved her, but she smiled vaguely in her sleep.

"See here, Durand, we want to stop this muddle before it makes more trouble," Jacob Garth greeted Price, as he walked up to the tent. Joao de Castro and Pasic were close behind him, nursing bruised faces, muttering unpleasantly together. Fouad followed, and a crowd of other men, whites and Arabs, most of them eyeing Price with unconcealed hostility.

Price stepped to meet them, trying to assume a confidence that he did not feel. "Of course," he agreed, "we don't want any trouble."

"You'll have to return Joao's woman," said Garth, his voice blandly sonorous, expressionless. His pouchy face, still tallow-white, as if the desert sun had never touched it, was blank as a mask. Unwinking, unfeeling, the small, pale eyes stared at Price.

"The girl isn't his property," Price stated, stiffly.

"*Dios!*" howled de Castro. "Do I pay for d' bitch, to 'ave heem rob me?"

Jacob Garth waved a puffy hand. "That's all right, Joao. We're going to settle this. . . . Durand, he did trade fairly for the woman. You can't appropriate her for yourself, in this high-handed way. The men won't stand for it."

"I don't propose," said Price, "to have the girl mistreated."

Garth moved ponderously forward, his voice rolled out persuasively:

"Listen, Durand. We're after big stakes. A fortune is wait-

82

ing for us. Many fortunes! A bigger strike than men have ever dreamed of. We've got to stand together; we can't afford a quarrel."

"I'm willing to do anything reasonable. I'll pay de Castro whatever you think he should have."

"It isn't a question of money. Not with the gold practically at our finger-tips. Surely you don't want to spoil our chances, for the sake of a woman. What's one native slut, against the loot of the golden land?"

"Please don't refer to her that way!" Price demanded, sharply. "After all, I'm the leader of this expedition. When I say hands off, it is hands off! De Castro is *not* going to have the girl!"

He was immediately sorry for the flare of anger, for it brought lowering looks from the men. To repair the damage, he turned to the little knot of whites and spoke pleadingly:

"See here, fellows, I want to do the right thing by all of you. I don't want to deal unfairly by de Castro. I'll give him my binoculars in place of those he traded for the girl. I don't want her for myself——"

Rude laughter broke out. Trying to hide his rising anger beneath a smile, he went on:

"Surely you don't want to see a helpless woman man-handled——"

"Enough of that," Garth cut in. "You must realize that these are men, not Sunday school children."

"Men, I hope, and not beasts."

His appeal met no sympathy. These were a hard sort: no other would have been attracted by this desperate raid into the desert's heart. Many of them were outside the law. Hardship and fear and greed had ridden down whatever of chivalry they might have had.

The faintest hint of a sardonic smile crossed Jacob Garth's placid, red-bearded face.

"Has it occurred to you, Durand," his question rolled out deliberately, "that you have just about lived out your usefulness as our leader? It's possible, you know, that we could do without you—now there are no more checks to be signed."

"The double-cross, eh?" said Price, scornfully.

Garth heaved his massive shoulders. "If you like. I came into this infernal desert for gold. I'm not going to let any native hussy stop me. Or any foolish convention."

"De Castro will not touch the girl," Price said evenly, in steel-cold tones, "so long as I am alive. *Now* what do you say?"

"I don't want any bloodshed, Durand. We'll make a peaceable bargain."

"What's that?"

"You can keep the jade tonight. I talked de Castro into letting you have her first. In the morning, you can turn her over to him."

"I'll do nothing of the kind."

"Think it over," Garth advised blandly. "If you don't decide to be reasonable, we'll take her. I'll hate to part company with you, Durand. You're a good man, and that's what we need. But you can't wreck the expedition. Think it over!"

8. "LA SIWA HU"

PRICE DURAND was not the kind who can surrender gracefully, even to overwhelming opposition. He had sometimes wished that he could give way meekly to circumstances as some men do; it would have made life, at times, much more convenient. But some obscure quirk, deep in his nature, made him a fighter. Resistance to his will had always roused in him a dogged determination not to yield.

Submission was left out of his nature. When opposed, it was impossible for him to do anything but fight, with every resource at his command. Nor was he given to weighing the consequences of defeat. His fatalistic faith in the Durand luck was supreme. And that luck had never failed—probably because invincible resourcefulness had never given it a chance.

When the men had gone, Price looked back into his tent. Aysa lay still upon the blankets, breathing quietly. Her oval face was half toward him, fresh, lovely, pomegranate lips a little parted. Long lashes lay on her cheeks, ruddy brown.

One glance was enough to steel his determination not to surrender her to the Macanese. His blood boiled at thought of such sleeping loveliness despoiled. No, he was not going to give her up. He had until morning to find some way to save her—unless Joao de Castro, in the meantime, found an opportunity to murder him.

The yellow moon, at the first quarter, hung near the zenith at dusk. Through the first half of the night, Price waited impatiently at his tent, near the slumbering, exhausted girl.

Golden Blood

Sam Sorrows had cheerfully offered to remain on guard, in the tank. Price accepted gratefully, and gave him, as a dubious token of appreciation, the key to the chest of gold in the tank. Price had decided to leave the caravan, with the girl; that seemed the only course open except disgraceful submission: two men could not fight the whole expedition.

The camp slowly fell into sleep, until the only movement was that of the regular sentries, two whites and two Arabs, pacing along their beats beyond the kneeling camels, hailing one another occasionally.

Near midnight the reddened moon sank beyond the dunes, its brief glow faded; and Price was ready to put his plan into action.

With a whispered word to Sam Sorrows, he slipped away into starlight darkness. Silently, he saddled his own camel, which was kneeling near, found two full skins of water and slung them to the high pommels, with a small bag of grain for the beast.

Returning to the tent, he packed his saddle-bags. Chocolate. Hard-tack. Dried meat. Rolls of the tough, dried apricot pulp which the Arabs call "mare's hide." Emergency medical kit. Binoculars. Extra ammunition for rifle and automatic.

When all was ready, he sat listening to the girl's regular breathing, reluctant to disturb her. At last he dared delay no longer. Gently he roused her, cautioning her to silence.

In complete darkness—for a light would have alarmed the camp—he gave her food and water. Sometimes his moving hands met hers; he found the contact vaguely exciting.

"The men with me say that I must give you back to him from whom I took you," he whispered. "I can not fight them all, so we are going away."

"Where?"

"To Anz, perhaps? You were going there."

"I was. But Anz is dead, a city of ghosts. No living man has even seen it." Her soft whisper went husky. "I do not want you to die, my protector. Let me go alone."

"No, I'm going along to look out for you. But don't talk about dying. You can count on the Durand luck."

"But my enemies are many—and strong. My own people will hunt me, to escape the wrath of the golden folk. And Malikar is seeking me upon the yellow tiger, pursuing me with . . . *the shadow!*"

"Let's go," said Price. Lifting the saddle-bags, he slipped from the tent. Aysa followed silently, clutching her golden dagger.

Price paused to bid Sam Sorrows a silent farewell, then guided the girl to his kneeling camel.

"Mount," he whispered.

"Wait," Aysa demurred. "Perhaps I can find my own animal. Listen!"

For minutes they stood still. The camp lay dark in the pallid light of the desert stars. Black tents looming here and there. Camels, kneeling or grotesquely sprawled. Dim forms of men sleeping in the open, wrapped only in their *abbas*.

A mysterious murmur of sound floated on the darkness. The breathing of men. The low, dismal groans of resting camels. The occasional tinkling of a camel-bell. The distant cries of the sentries. It all had a strange undertone, for the dawn-wind had risen, and creeping sand whispered across

87

the dunes beyond the camp, with a muted and eery susur-
ration.

Aysa moved suddenly, murmured, "The bell of my camel!"

Noiselessly she slipped away in the darkness, guided by
the faint tinkle that Price had not even heard.

He started to follow, alarmed. Then he came back to
his own mount, stood tense, listening, waiting. The subdued and slumberous noises of the camp drifted about him,
and the faint dry sibilance of moving sand, as if the ghosts
of this dead land had been wakened by the dawn-wind.

Price had not realized the hold that Aysa, in a few brief
hours, had gained upon his feelings, until Nur's harsh
scream of alarm splintered the murmurous silence of the
somnolent camp. The sound stabbed him like a blade. He
felt weakness, almost physical sickness, of fear and despair.
For a moment he was trembling, shaken with such a chill
of fear for the girl's sake as he had never felt for his
own.

Then strength and determination flowed back into him. He
leapt into the saddle of his camel, hastened it to its feet,
snatched out his automatic.

The Arab Nur, he realized, must have been sleeping
near his newly acquired camel, and had been roused as
Aysa prepared to mount the animal.

Instantly the camp was in uproar. Men sprang up, shouting. Camels grumbled in alarm, leapt up and ran about,
three-legged. Flashlight beams burst from the tents of the
whites. Reports of wildly fired guns punctuated astonished
curses in several European tongues, and impassioned ap-
peals to Allah in the name of his prophet.

Through the confusion a white dromedary came dashing,

Aysa clinging to it, flourishing the golden dagger with which she must have cut its hobbles.

"*Aiee*, Price Durand!" her voice pealed, and Price thought there was eager exultation in it.

Price swung his *hejin* in beside her own, racing toward the edge of the camp.

"*Shayton el Kabir!*" Nur shrieked behind them. "My camel! *Effendi* Duran and the woman!"

Calm, reverberant, Jacob Garth's voice rang out in a command to the sentries: "Muller! Mawson! Stop them!"

A bullet hummed close to Price's ears, and he heard the shrill, excited screaming of Joao de Castro: "Catch heem! D' thief!"

Price and Aysa plunged through the outskirts of the camp. The sentries, on foot, ran toward them, sought them with flashlight beams, fired wildly.

"Lean low," Price called to the girl, "and ride!"

A little breathless laugh answered him. And her clear voice pealed out in a mocking farewell to her enemies, "*Wa' salem!*"

"Mount!" the old sheikh Fouad howled behind them. "*Bismillah!* Pursue them."

"I geef my rifle," de Castro shouted, "to 'ooever bring back d' bitch!"

Riding side by side, the two were well beyond the sentries. Before them lay mystic, starlit desert. They raced their camels for the tawny darkness.

Behind came a confusion of shouts, the "*Yahh! Yahh!*" of men urging on the mounts, the swift thudding of many feet.

Price turned in his saddle. Faintly, by starlight, he could see the dark mass of the pursuers, only a few hundred yards

89

behind. Half the camp was following, spreading out in a great fan.

His heart sank in despair. There was little chance of escape, he knew, with their followers so near. Even if they could evade capture until daylight, the Arabs, skilled in the art of *asar*, or enemy-tracking, would soon hunt them down.

Still running side by side, they topped the first dune. In the moment they were silhouetted against the stars, a scattered volley of shots crackled behind them.

As their mounts ran down the slope, Price did a thing that surprized himself. Leaning toward the girl, he called:

"Aysa of the golden land, I must tell you something now, because I'll never have another chance. You are beautiful—and brave!"

The girl laughed. "They'll never catch us. We have all the desert! They are dogs hunting eagles!"

Then he heard the bellow of the tank's engine, as it burst into roaring life; the clangor of its metal treads as it thundered across the rocky plain; the clattering music of its guns.

Could the old Kansan be joining their pursuers? Of course not! Sam Sorrows was doing the one thing that could save them.

"Good old Sam!" Price cried. "Giving them something else to worry over."

The Arabs, he knew, still held their deadly fear of the tank. Its lumbering charge into their midst would scatter them in frantic terror. And none of the whites yet rode well enough to be a serious menace.

Whine of motor, rattle of guns and outcry of men were faint behind when they topped the second long dune. Beyond the third, and the only sound was the dry rustle of creeping sand in the cool dawn-wind, ghost-murmurings of the dead world about them.

The first red glow of Arabian day found the two alone, still riding side by side. Their weary camels were plodding slowly across a dead plain of alkali that crunched underfoot with a sound like crushed snow.

Ahead lay another drear range of bare, irregular red-sand dunes, bloody in the sunrise. Vast, terrible horizons surrounded them. Low, far black hills, granite skeletons of ancient mountains. Billowing miles of dead drift-sand. Lifeless saltpans, shimmering ghosts of the lakes they once had been.

Already the smoky horizons quivered in unending undulations of heat, and the silvery mock-lakes of the morning mirage flowed across the flickering, infernal plains, rippling in tantalizing promises of cool refreshment, fleeing away to merge into the bright sky.

The camp was many miles behind, and the rustling sands of the dawn-wind had already obscured their trail. They had lost even the caravan road that was marked with skulls. They were two alone, with the tawny and unconquerable wilderness, fighting the deadly, hostile loneliness of the Empty Abode.

"*La Siwa Hu*," Price murmured a name of the Arabs for the desert, which means "Where there is none but Him."

9. THE CITY OF THE SANDS

IN THE evening of the third day they were toiling across an endless, billowing ocean of yellow-red sand. Camels near dead, water-skins almost empty, Price and Aysa rode on, in quest of ancient Anz. Their mouths were dry, and they did not often speak, for the parching air was like hot sand in the throat. But Price looked often at the girl, clinging to her *hejin* wearily but with invincible determination.

The oval face beneath her white *kafiyeh* was blistered, the full lips cracked and bleeding from sun and alkali dust, the tired violet eyes inflamed by the pressure of glaring light. But still Aysa was beautiful, and she smiled at him with courage on her weary face.

Cruel, those three days had been. Yet Price regretted them only for the hardship the girl had so stoically suffered. An odd contentment filled him; his old, bitter *ennui* was dead. Aysa's companionship had become a precious thing, worth the living of a life.

She was the guide, finding the way by obscure landmarks that she knew by tradition alone. At sunset she turned to him, troubled.

"Anz should be before us," she whispered, husky with thirst. "We should have seen it from the last ridge."

"Don't worry, little one!" He had tried to speak cheerfully, but his voice croaked false and hollow. "We'll find it."

"Anz should be right here," she insisted. "My father taught me the signs, before he died, as his father taught him. It should be here."

Perhaps, Price thought, the lost city *was* here. According to Aysa's story, none of her people had seen it for a thousand years. It might be beneath them, completely buried! But he kept the thought to himself.

"Let's ride on," he said. And he pretended to discover with surprize the few drops of water in the goatskin—his own share, which he had saved when they last drank. After a single sparing sip, she suspected the subterfuge and would take no more.

They goaded the weary camels on, as the inflamed, sullen eye of the sun went out. And still they went on, in an eldritch world of pallid moonlight, sometimes walking and driving the exhausted animals, until they collapsed of thrist and fatigue and despair, to sleep fitfully.

Dawn came and they saw Anz.

The black walls, of Cyclopean basalt blocks, stood half a mile away. Driven sands of ages had scored in them deep furrows. Here and there they had tumbled into colossal ruin, like a breakwater broken by the yellow sea of sand. Tawny, billowing dunes were piled against them in crested waves, sometimes completely covering them. Shattered ruins rose within the walls, crumbling, half buried, darkly mysterious in the dawn, emerging grim and desolate from night's shadows as if from the mists of centuries immemorial.

Price roused Aysa to point it out. But his hopes sank swiftly after the first thrill of discovery. Anz was truly a city of death, sand-shrouded, forgotten. Little chance he thought, of finding in this dark necropolis the water for which every tissue of their bodies screamed.

Aysa was filled with new eagerness.

"Then I was not lost," she cried. "Let us enter the walls!"

They urged the unwilling camels to their feet, and toiled toward Anz.

Black walls breasted the conquering sand, massive, forbidding. The gates, mighty panels of patina-darkened bronze, were closed between their guarding towers, red sand banked so high against them that a thousand men could not have pushed them open.

Driving the staggering camels to the crest of a dune that had overflowed the wall, they saw the city within. A city strange as a dream. A dead city, buried in sand.

A ruined and leaning tower rose here above the red dust, like the end of a rotting bone. A shattered dome of white marble, there, like an age-bleached skull. Or a cupola of corroded metal, above some buried building.

Over the silent mounds of the sand-beleaguered city Price sensed a brooding spirit of slumberous antiquity, a clinging ghost of the forgotten past. One instant, in imagination, he saw the ruined buildings whole again, saw the broad streets cleared of sand, magnificent thoroughfares thronged with multitudes. He saw Anz as it once had been, before dead Petra was carved from the rocks of Edom, before Babylon rose upon the Euphrates, before the first pharaohs reared their enduring mausoleums upon the Nile.

One moment he saw Anz living. Then its sand-conquered, time-shattered wreck smote him with a melancholy sense of death and dissolution.

Aysa sighed hopelessly.

"Then the prophecy is a jest," she whispered. "Anz is truly dead. Iru could not be waiting here! 'Tis a city of the sands!"

"But we may find water." Price tried to seem hopeful. "There must be wells, or reservoirs."

They made the camels slide down the dune, into the old city, and began the weary and search of its forest of ruins.

It was near noon when they approached a huge pile of shattered marble, standing upon a vast platform of titanic basalt blocks, not yet completely covered by the sifting sand. The flagging camels refused to climb the yielding sand-slopes to the platform, and they left them, to explore the building in search of a well.

Price afterward cursed himself for not taking his rifle and the holster containing his automatic, which were slung to the pommels of his saddle. But he was almost too weary to stand. And Anz appeared so completely a city of the dead he had no thought of living enemies.

They clambered to the crumbling platform, and stood beneath a broken colonnade. Aysa studied a half-obliterated inscription on the architrave, turned to Price with weary eagerness, whispering:

"This is the palace of Iru! The king of the legend, who sleeps."

They passed the columns, entered the arched gateway to the palace courtyard.

"Al Hamdu Lillah!" breathed Price, incredulous.

In the court, surrounded by high walls that the sand had not overwhelmed, their senses were struck by the cool green fragrance of a sunken garden. Within the inclosure was a tiny, bright oasis, a wondrous tropic garden in the heart of grimmest desolation, richly and blessedly green.

With sweetest music, crystal water trickled from a stone-rimmed fountain at the end of the court, to spread among a thick jungle of date-palms and fig-trees, of pomegranates and vines and fragrant-flowering shrubs.

The garden was wild, untended. For a thousand years, by Aysa's story, no human being had seen it; these plants must have propagated themselves for generations.

For a moment Price was unbelieving. This wonder of greenery, this song of falling water, was impossible! Stuff of desert-fevered dreams.

Then with a hoarse, gasping cry, he took Aysa by the arm, and they ran down the crumbling granite steps, un-used for a thousand years, to the floor of the hidden gar-den. Together, they fell on their knees at the fountain's lip, rinsed bitter dust from their mouths, drank deep of sweet cool water.

To Price the next hour was a glad dream; a mad riot of delicious sensation, of drinking clear water, of laving the stinging desert grime from his drawn body, of filling him-self with fresh, delightful fruits, of resting beside joyous, laughing Aysa in soothing green shade.

Then he remembered the camels, and they went out to-gether to bring the exhausted beasts into this desert para-dise. An involuntary cry of dismay broke from Price's lips as he came to the edge of the basalt platform, and looked down upon the kneeling *hejins*.

The animals were where they had been left. But the saddlebags had been torn open, contents ransacked, part of it scattered about over the sand. The rifle and the automatic, which Price had left slung to his saddle, were gone.

10. IN THE CRYPTS OF ANZ

HE pillaging of the saddle-bags remained a mystery. Peering about the dead city, after he made the discovery, Price was able to see no living being. Utter silence clung to him, tense, expectant . . . but nothing happened.

Pushing away their sense of lurking danger, Price and Aysa presently returned their attention to the camels.With some difficulty, Aysa tugging at the halter-ropes, Price pushing and goading from the rear, they got the animals one by one upon the platform, and turned them into the sunken garden.

Then Price took Aysa's golden dagger, their only remaining weapon, and cut himself a heavy club, in the garden.

They rested, lying beside the fountain, until sunset, and then ventured out again to find what had become of the pilfered weapons. Somewhat refreshed, and driven by haunting fear, they thoroughly explored the sand-heaped, crumbling piles of the lost city, without finding any inhabitants, or, indeed, any habitable place.

Yet there was no denying that the guns were gone.

In the dusk they were returning to the sunken garden when Aysa seized Price's shoulder in a grasp nerved with terror, and pointed silently.

A strange figure was darting away from the colonnade before the entrance—a tall man, lean as a desert Arab, attired in a long, hooded, burnoose-like robe that was a peculiar shade of blue. As he ran along the platform, sprang off into the sand, Price saw that he carried the stolen rifle.

A moment he paused, looking back. On his forehead, above his cruel, hatchet face, was a glittering golden brand, the yellow likeness of a coiled serpent. Then he vanished, beyond a broken column.

"A snake-man," whispered Aysa, her voice muted with fear.

"A what?" Price took her trembling hand, looked into her distressed violet eyes.

"A slave of the snake, under Malikar. The golden man must have known of the prophecy that a woman named Aysa would wake Iru. He guessed that I had fled to Anz, and sent the priest here to capture me."

Price was staring at her in some astonishment. Aysa frightened was a new experience to him. As the helpless prisoner of the Macanese she had revealed no fear. He was shocked to see her white-faced, trembling, her violet eyes wide and sick with terror.

While he himself was much disturbed by the loss of the weapons, he did not believe they were in immediate danger. The blue-robe had fled from them.

"Buck up, kid," he told her. "It can't be that bad. When everything else goes wrong, we still have the Durand luck."

She moved toward him a little, and he put his arm around her, still peering alertly into the gloom swift-falling upon the shattered skeleton of the lost city. She drew herself against him with an eager little movement, murmuring softly *"M'alme!"*

From that time until the end she was apprehensive, fearful. Shadows of strange dread lurked always in her violet eyes. She tried to forget, to laugh with Price. But her gayety was strained, unnatural, feverish.

99

A week went by, and the snake-man was seen no more. The two were so near supreme happiness! The oasis was a garden of wonder, supplying all physical needs. They would have been content to forget the outer world, dwell there for ever. Each found in the other a joy never known before, a bliss made only more keenly poignant by the intruding darkness of anxiety.

In the rear wall of the courtyard was the arched entrance to a long hall of granite, that led back into the sand-heaped, crumbling main pile of the old palace. Near the garden it was bright enough, illuminated by high, unglazed clerestory windows. Farther back, however, the invading sand had completely covered it. It became a dark tunnel into mysterious buried ruin.

They had explored it as far as daylight penetrated, and since it furnished the only standing roof available, they made the outer end of it their dwelling.

Above the end of the hall was a stone tower, still standing, so high that it overlooked the walls of Anz. Price was able to climb its crumbling stairs. Several times daily he ascended, to scan the ruins of Anz and the surrounding desert for Aysa's enemies.

On the morning of the ninth day Price saw a tiny speck creeping across the heaving oceans of yellow-reddish dunes, northward. He watched it for an hour, until it had grown to a tiny yellow animal, with a black dot upon its back, running toward the buried city.

"I see that yellow tiger coming," he told Aysa, when he rejoined her in the green shadows of the marble-walled garden.

He could see that the information threw her into an extremity of terror. Her face went white, and she trembled, though she retained her composure.

"It's Malikar!" she whispered, "riding himself after me, upon the tiger. *M'alme*, we must hide! With your weapons gone, we can not fight the golden man! Where——"

Price nodded toward the end of the long hall.

"What about that? I've been wanting to explore it, anyhow."

The girl shook her head. "No, we would be trapped there, in the dark." Then another idea evidently overtook her. "But no matter!" she cried. "Let us hasten!"

Each gathered an armful of the rude torches they had made—merely bundles of dried palm-leaves. And they set out down the hall.

The floor, sifted with red sand, was twenty feet wide; the arched roof thirty feet above. For many yards there was light enough from the entrance and the high windows. Then they entered the main pile of the palace, a mountain of tumbled, sand-covered ruin.

Lighting the torches, they went on, through the darkness and the utter silence of a city entombed. Their feet trod soundlessly upon the sand; instinctively they spoke only in whispers.

Dark, narrower passages opened at intervals from the long central hall. They paused to peer down each. Most of them were filled with sand that had sifted from above; a few were blocked with fallen masonry.

At last, hundreds of feet from the entrance, the central hall ended in a blank stone wall. Price was discouraged;

they had found neither hiding-place nor fortress; the hall seemed only a gloomy trap. Aysa eagerly led the way into the last branching passage.

It was a smaller, lower hall, almost free of sand. They had followed it a hundred feet when they passed a pile of moldering wood that once had been a door. Beyond, a steep flight of steps led downward. Complete darkness and breathless silence mocked them from below.

Price could not keep his imagination from conjuring up weird fantasms, upon that black stair, leading into the bowels of a city that had been lost a thousand years. He hesitated, went on only when Aysa moved to pass him.

Three hundred steps downward, and they entered the crypts.

A gloomy labyrinth beneath the buried city; long halls, intricately winding, hewn in dark rock. The stagnant air was dank, laden with dusty odors of the tomb, but not actually dangerous, Price knew, since the torches continued to flare.

They stopped at the foot of the stair, peered rather apprehensively about. The torches were far too feeble to illuminate the vast chambers. Grotesque shadows flickered, leapt at them like dancing demons.

"I believe I'd rather meet Malikar outside," Price whispered. "Suppose the torches went out!"

Shadows danced like demons in the winding, pillared halls, and a taunting echo mocked ". . . *the torches went out* . . ."

"We are in the crypts of Anz!" Aysa cried. "The tombs of the ancient great ones! Iru is sleeping here!"

Ghostly echoes whispered ". . . *Iru is sleeping here* . . ."

Price shuddered. Above ground, in daylight, it had been easy enough to laugh at the prophecy that an ancient king would wake again; but in these dank, uncanny catacombs, whose lurking darkness was always leaping to battle with the torchlight, the thing seemed grimly possible.

Rather reluctantly, Price accompanied Aysa as he began a circuit of the walls, pausing to study the inscriptions upon the narrow, upright slabs of dark stone that were the doors of tombs.

"The vault of Iru!" she cried suddenly, and Price started.

It was a low, narrow door of stone, with a knob of dull gold. She turned the knob, motioned Price to set his shoulder to it. He hesitated, and she moved to try her own strength with it.

The door swung inward upon silent hinges, when he lunged against it, more easily than he had expected. He fell into the tomb. Aysa followed anxiously, in response to his startled cry. It was a small, square chamber, hewn in dark rock. On a long, shelf-like niche in the farther wall were the remains of Iru.

To Price's relief, the old king was extremely dead. Only the bare skeleton remained.

On the end of the ledge lay his weapons: a folded skirt of chain-mail, the interlocking links golden, finely wrought; a small, oval shield to be carried on the left arm; and a great battle-ax.

Eagerly, Price picked up the ax: here, at least, was a weapon. The heavy, massive head was gold, untarnished. Its keen, curving blade, half as long as the handle, was engraved, like the sword of tempered gold in Jacob Garth's possession, with inscriptions in a language Price could not read.

The short, thick helve was of ebony, or some similar black, hard wood. It seemed perfectly preserved. Worn or carved on it was the impression of a hand, a rounded groove for each finger.

Price lifted it, as if to swing it. And those grooves fitted his fingers perfectly, as if the ax were made for his hand, not that of the skeleton beside him, dead a thousand years and more.

"Queer," he muttered. "Just fits my hand."

"Even so," Aysa whispered. "It is strange—or is it strange?"

Puzzled by something in her voice, he looked up at the girl. She stood just within the tiny, rock-hewn tomb, the flaring torches in her hands. She was smiling, framed against the blackness of the crypts, her violet eyes suddenly mysterious with some enigmatic thought.

Price had never seen her so beautiful as there against the gloom of the catacombs. The sheer loveliness of her made his heart ache; made him want to take her in his arms again, and kiss her; made him want desperately to carry her away from the weird perils gathering about them, to some far place of security and peace.

"Let's get out of here," he muttered.

Aysa turned, and stopped with a horrified gasp, as the torch-light fell upon a man in the doorway behind her—a tall, hatchet-faced man, upon whose high forehead glittered the golden likeness of a coiled serpent!

Price leapt at the intruder, whirling the golden battle-ax, which he still had been carrying in his hand. And if Aysa had displayed fright, the snake-man betrayed abject terror. His mouth fell open. His thin, cruel features were distorted with the utmost horror that Price had ever seen upon a human face. Shrieking, hands flung up, he staggered backward, and ran into the black, labyrinthine catacombs."

"A slave of the snake," Aysa whispered. "Malikar sent him down to search for me."

"What scared him so? He looked as if he'd seen—I don't know what!"

"I think I know," Aysa said quietly. "He saw Iru awakened."

"Iru awakened? What do you mean?"

"In you the prophecy is fulfilled!" she cried her, eyes shining. "You are Iru, come back to conquer the golden folk and deliver the Beni Anz!"

"I? Of course not! Nonsense!"

"Why not? You are tall, as Iru was, red-haired, blue-eyed. Did not the ax fit your hand?"

It *was* something of a coincidence. But Price had always looked askance upon theories of reincarnation. He felt that one life was load enough, without attempting to assume the burdens of the dead.

"Anyhow," Aysa added practically, "it will help for the snake-man to think you are Iru. Why not put on the mail?"

"I'll be anything, sweetheart," Price assured her, "to get you out of this."

"And perhaps you should learn the ax-song, written on

105

the blade," she suggested. "Iru always sang it in battle."

By torchlight, she read the words to him. Their strange, chanting rhythm oddly stirred his blood. He could render them only roughly into English:

> *Hew —*
> *Justice in battle!*
> *Foe of all evil!*
>
> *Strike —*
> *Child of the anvil!*
> *Forged by the thunder!*
>
> *Cleave —*
> *Korlu the smiter!*
> *Lightning-tempered!*
>
> *Slay —*
> *Korlu the war-ax!*
> *Drinker of life-blood!*
>
> *Kill —*
> *Korlu the red doom!*
> *Keeper of death-gate!*

Price donned the yellow mail. Upon his unaccustomed body it felt cold and stiff and heavy, but it fitted extraordinarily well. He took up the small, oval shield, and fiercely gripped the helve of the ax.

He had never loved Aysa more than during the bitter time of that weird vigil in Iru's tomb, when the cold dank air of the catacombs brushed like clammy wings against them, and minutes stretched into hours, as they awaited the coming of Malikar, sitting side by side.

Greenish light flickered down the stair, and five men came into the crypts. Four were blue-robed, hooded figures; two armed with long pikes, two carrying torches that flared strangely green.

The other was the golden man Price had seen on the tiger. Gigantic, thick of shoulder, mighty of arm. He wore a red skull-cap, a volumnious robe of crimson. On his shoulder he carried his great, spiked club of yellow metal.

He led his men straight toward the tomb of Iru.

Triumphant evil rode his harshly lined, golden-bearded yellow face. Ugly elation gleamed in his shallow eyes. Eyes of unhuman age and wisdom, brooding with dark secrets of the lost past.

Price waited in the tomb, gripping the ancient ax.

The blue-robes, he saw, were afraid. Their steps dragged. Their faces were white and apprehensive. Malikar pushed roughly past them, but even he stopped outside the tomb.

"Come forth, woman!" he shouted harshly.

Aysa made no reply.

The yellow man snatched a torch from one of his cowering men, and pushed boldly into the tomb. Price stepped to meet him in the doorway.

The flat yellow eyes held fear for a moment, incredulous amazement. Then Malikar leered grimly, came on.

"*Kalb ibn kalb!*" he snarled, in the same oddly accented Arabic that Aysa spoke. "Iru can not rest? *I* can put him back to sleep!"

He flung the flambeau to the floor between them, where its green flame still flared, unextinguished. In both hands he lifted the great spiked mace.

107

Golden Blood

Price struck with the yellow ax, a short, chopping swing at the red skull-cap. The golden man stepped quickly back, into the shelter of the doorway. The shimmering ax-blade slipped harmlessly in front of his face, but his own blow was diverted; he could not swing the mace in the narrow doorway.

The golden man charged through the opening again, and Price began chanting the ax-song Aysa had taught him. Once more he saw fear in the shallow, tawny eyes. From one of the blue-robes came a shaken cry of terror.

After an instant's hesitation, Malikar leapt into the tomb.

Moving to the rhythm of his chant, Price gave ground before the threatening mace, whirled the battle-ax aloft, put all his strength into a swing at the red skull-cap. Put too much strength into the blow!

He felt the ominous cracking of the age-dried helve, as the ax came down, knew in an instant of sickening tragedy what had happened.

A fatal snap, and the haft was light in his hands, a useless, brittle stick. The broad-edged head clattered to the floor of the tomb, as Price fell back in dismay, the ax-song dead.

A queer, hurt feeling was in his heart. He had been betrayed. The Durand luck had failed him.

An unpleasant grin of surprised triumph on his yellow face, Malikar sprang forward, lifting his great, spiked club deliberately, to crush the skull of his disarmed foe.

With a sharp little cry of pain and rage, Aysa leapt forward, under the descending mace. The slender dagger flashed in her hands.

108

Malikar checked the blow, reached out a massive, red-sleeved, golden arm, seized her lifted wrist. The dagger clattered from her helpless fingers, and Malikar flung her, with careless, brutal strength, toward the waiting blue-robes beyond the door.

Price sprang at the yellow man, swinging a blow with his fist. The mace came down over his head. It was a short, one-armed blow. And Price ducked, flung up the oval shield. The mace crashed through his defense, and splintering fire exploded in his head.

Price sat up in the cold, musty darkness of the subterranean tomb. The torches were gone. He was very thirsty; in his dry mouth was a bitter, metallic taste. He knew that he had been unconscious for many hours.

He fumbled about. No other living thing was in the tomb. But he struck something large and smooth and imperfectly round, that rolled rattling across the floor.

Fighting down icy panic, he stumbled to the doorway. A smooth, unbroken, surface of cold stone opposed him. Wildly, he ran his fingers over the tight-fitting slab. Then he remembered that the massive stone door of the vault had swung inward, and that it had no knob on the inside.

He was sealed in Iru's tomb!

11. THE TIGER'S TRAIL

AFTER a time Price gave up his frantic attempts to force the vault's locked door, and sank back exhausted on the chill stone floor of the ancient tomb.

Panic was near, the red, blind insanity of terror. His body was a-tremble, clammy with sudden sweat. He found himself beating with his hands on the polished cold stone, and the vault was full of his hoarse, useless shouts.

A quiet voice in his brain bade him sit down, and conserve his strength, and think. His situation was extreme, almost melodramatic—locked in a tomb, in the catacombs beneath Anz, beneath a sand-whelmed city centuries lost. Fear-nerved struggles would get him nowhere. He must collect his scattered senses, think.

He dared not hope for outside aid. Malikar and his acolytes, departing with the captive Aysa, had obviously left him here to die. The vault must be opened by his own efforts. And he had not long for the task; the air was already vitiated. His lungs were gasping in the musty stuff with great gulps; his head rang and roared. Already half suffocated, he was still dazed from Malikar's final blow.

Pressing his hands to his throbbing head, Price tried to think. He must take stock of his prison. If he could find some tool . . .

Anxiously he fumbled for his matches, felt the little box. With a sign of relief he struck a light, peered about the tiny square chamber. Among scattered human bones he saw the broken helve of the ax, then the shining golden head of it,

112

at the door. The oval shield was near, the heavy yellow mail still upon his body.

Abruptly giddy from the splitting pain in his head, he leaned on the cold wall, and lighted a cigarette with the dying match. The smoke cleared his brain a little; it hid the musty charnel odor of the vault. But still his head throbbed, still his mouth was bitter and dry.

When the cigarette was gone he lit another match, and examined the door, a massive slab of hewn and polished granite, cleverly hung, so that metal lock and hinges were concealed. On the outside there was a golden knob. But its smooth black inner surface was unbroken.

Forcing himself to deliberate and unhurried movement, he picked up the head of the golden ax. Wrapping his handkerchief about the blade to protect his fingers, he attacked the door with the picklike point opposite the cutting edge.

The hidden mechanism of the lock, he reasoned, must be contained in a cavity of the stone, at the level of the golden knob. The shell of granite covering it would be relatively thin; it might be possible to break it away.

The stone was obdurate, his tool clumsy. His head drummed with pain, and the air was rapidly becoming unbreathable. Gasping for breath, he reeled as he worked, occasionally striking a match to estimate his progress.

For a time that seemed hours he toiled, when another man might have cursed and dropped his tool and flung himself down to die. The idea of defeat, of failure, was not in Price Durand's nature. He had a vast confidence that the Durand luck—though it had so recently betrayed him— would come to his rescue, if he just kept fighting.

Thought of Aysa, as much as his own safety, spurred him on. He knew that he loved the brown-haired, gayly brave fugitive. She was his, by some immutable law of life. Her captivity filled him with savage resentment.

Ringing hollow beneath the ax-point, the shell of rock cracked at last. Rapidly, then, it crumbled beneath his blows. Holding a match in one hand, he manipulated the bronze levers and tumblers of the ancient lock.

Staggering and blind with fatigue and asphyxiation, he slid back the great bolt, swung the door inward, and pitched through the opening into the cleaner air of the open catacombs.

In delirious joy he sucked in air that had once seemed musty and stale, until he was able to light one of the torches he and Aysa had brought into the crypts. Then taking up the ax and the oval shield, he found the stair, and climbed wearily back to the surface.

Price laughed weakly and uncertainly, for pure joy, when he came into the hot, white noonday light of the hidden garden. He stood a while in the sun, half blind, drinking up the blazing radiance, the warm fresh air.

Presently he stumbled to the fountain and washed his mouth and drank. Collapsing upon the grass beside the pool, he dropped into the sleep of complete exhaustion.

Upon the dawn of a clear, still day, he woke, ravenously hungry. His head was clear again, the bruise of Malikar's mace subsiding. As he found food from the slender remaining store, and ate, his mind was busy with the problem of Aysa's rescue.

It was characteristic of Price that he did not pause to wonder whether he could liberate the girl. His only problem was *how*.

It was in the soft earth where water had overflowed from the pool that he found the tiger's tracks. At first he could not think what had made them, they were so amazingly huge. Though shaped like those of any cat, they were large as an elephant's.

Eagerly he followed the deep prints along the side of the garden, out of the walled court, and off among the sand-heaped ruins of Anz. The wind had not yet moved sufficient sand to efface them.

At once he determined to follow the tiger's trail. That, surely, would be the shortest path to Aysa. He did not pause to reflect upon the dangers and difficulties that might lie before him, except in order to prepare to meet them.

Delay would mean disaster. The loose red sand, flowing almost like a liquid beneath the wind, would soon obliterate the prints. But he had to make a few preparations before taking the trail.

First he searched the oasis for a stick of hardwood, carved out a new helve and fitted it to the golden ax, now his only weapon.

Then he saddled the two camels, which had regained much of their lost strength upon the lush vegetation of the oasis, and packed the full water-skins, and a bundle of green forage, upon Aysa's beast.

Mounting his own *hejin* and leading the other, he rode out of the hidden oasis where he had found the zenith of happiness and the nadir of despair, rode through the shattered piles of sand-leaguered Anz, and over a yellow-red dune that had conquered the black walls.

All day he followed the gigantic tracks. Straight northward they led him, across a billowing sea of crescent hills. The trail, at first, was easy enough to follow. But in the blazing afternoon a breath of wind arose, furnace-hot, and the obliterating drift-sand crept rustling before it.

By sunset the trail was hardly distinguishable. A dozen times Price lost it on the upward slope of a dune, only to pick it up again in the hollow beyond. At dusk he had to stop.

The camels were weary. They had not completely recovered from the terrible journey to Anz. And Price, in his desperate haste, had urged them on unsparingly. He fed them the green forage, ate and drank meagerly, and rolled himself in his blanket, praying that the wind would stop.

It blew harder, instead. All night dry sands whispered with the desert's ghostly voice, mockingly, as if they taunted Price with Aysa's fate at the hands of the golden Malikar. Long before dawn the trail was swept out completely.

Before sunrise Price saddled the *hejins* again, and rode on in the same direction that the trail had led him, driving the jaded animals to the limit of their endurance.

That afternoon his own mount fell down upon the hot sand and died. He gave most of the remaining water to Aysa's dromedary, and rode on, into the unknown north. From the next dune he looked back at the white shape sprawled in the sun . . . a hardy beast; it had served him well and he regretted to leave so . . . and he rode on over the crest.

Some time on the next day—the shadow of the desert's madness was already descending upon him; he never remembered whether it was morning or afternoon—he came out of the dunes, upon a vast flat plain of yellow clay.

Upon that, he reasoned with the dull effort that precedes delirium, the giant tracks would not have been obliterated by the wind. After an hour's riding back and forth, he found the enormous prints again, and followed them doggedly across the clay-pan.

The water was all gone that night. He lay down near the camel, in a dry *wadi.* His mouth was swollen and dry; he was too thirsty to sleep. But even if he could not sleep, he dreamed. Dreamed that he was back with Aysa at the lost oasis, drinking from the stone-rimmed pools and plucking fresh fruit. The dreams verged oddly into reality. He caught himself speaking to Aysa, and woke again with a start to his desolate surroundings.

Day came, and he rode on. The fevered dreams did not stop. He was back in Anz, with the lovely Aysa. He was with her in the deep tomb of Iru, fighting Malikar. He was back in the camp on the road of skulls freeing her from the clutches of Joao de Castro.

But through all the visions of his half-delirium, a single idea reigned in his spinning brain. A fixed purpose dominated him. And he urged the flagging camel northward, along the trail of a gigantic tiger.

Again the trail became more difficult to follow. The clay was flinty, harder; the great feet had left but slight impressions. In the afternoon the hard yellow pan gave way to bare black lava, to a flat, volcanic plateau whose sharp-edged, fire-twisted rocks were hard going for the foot-sore camel, and upon which the golden tiger had left no mark.

There the tracks were hopelessly lost. Price abandoned any attempt to find traces of the huge pads, and rode straight on over the rocky terrain, into the north. Night came, and moonless darkness. And still he urged the half-dead dromedary on, toward the pole-star, glittering pale above the desert horizon.

Polaris danced and beckoned and taunted. Strange pageantries of madness appeared and dissolved upon the star-lit desert. And Price rode on. Sometimes he forgot the reason, and wondered what he would find beneath the star. But still he rode on.

12. "THE ROCK OF HELL"

PRICE woke in the dawn, chilled and shivering beneath his blanket. The emaciated *hejin* sprawled beside him. He staggered to his feet, trying in vain to recall when he had stopped; and saw the mountain.

In the cold, motionless desert air, it looked very near, only a few miles across the barren, black volcanic plain, a mountain shaped like a truncated cone, rugged, steep-walled. On its summit was a bright coronal, a golden crest that exploded into scintillant splendor when the first sunlight touched it.

Price feared at first that it was mirage or delirium; but complete sanity had come back to him for a little while, with the chill of the dawn, and he knew the mountain was no dream. And it was too early for mirage; the mountain was too motionlessly real.

He remembered the old Arab's story of a black mountain, *Hajar Jehannum,* or "Rock of Hell," upon which golden *djinn* dwelt in a palace of yellow metal.

The parchment of Quadra y Vargas, the old Spanish soldier of fortune, came back to his mind, with its fantastic account of golden folk—"idols of gold that live and move"—dwelling upon a mountain in *la casa dorada,* and worshipped like gods by the people of the oasis below.

It had all seemed impossible. But he had seen the golden tiger, and its yellow riders, had fought with Malikar, and followed the tiger's trail for grim long days. Now here was the mountain, with its crown of gold. Impossible. But was it, like so many impossible things, true?

119

He goaded the staggering, grumbling *hejin* to its feet, climbed into the saddle, and rode on, toward the mountain. Aysa had been taken there, he knew, upon the golden tiger, by her yellow captor. And there he was going after her. It might not be easy to find her and set her free, but he was going to do it. If he himself failed, there was yet the Durand luck.

All day he went on toward the mountain. Sometimes the camel reeled and staggered. Then he dismounted and stumbled along on foot, driving it for a distance, until it could rest.

The grim lava tableland seemed to stretch out as he advanced. But at sunset he could distinguish the towers and spires of the glittering castle, shimmering, splendid, drawing him with resistless fascination.

Once more he toiled on, far into the night. At dawn the black rock seemed no nearer, but merely larger. Its black walls, of columnar basalt, frowned precipitously grim. They seemed unscalable. Price, in the more lucid periods of his brain-fevered advance, wondered how the castle could be reached.

A crenelated wall of black stone skirted the top of the cliffs—a wall apparently useless, for half a mile of sheer precipice hung below it. Within rose the piles of the unattainable castle. The blazing fulgor of gold, and the brilliant white of alabaster. Twisted domes and turrets. Slim towers. Balconied minarets. Broad roofs and pointed spires. Yellow gold, and white marble.

The high castle was not all of gold. But even so, the value of the yellow metal blazing from it was incalculable, Price knew. The treasure before his eyes might rival in value the monetary gold in the vaults of all the world.

But gold meant nothing, now, to Price Durand. He was fighting back the mists of madness, battling vision and delirium, ignoring the tortures of exhaustion, of thirst that parched his whole body. He was seeking a girl. A girl with gay violet eyes, whose name was Aysa.

Again he was riding on. The bloody, implacable sun rose once more, on his right, and flooded the lava plain with cruel light. The brief sanity of the dawn deserted, and madness of thirst rode back upon stinging barbs of radiation.

It was some time later in the day that the *hejin* lifted its white, snake-like neck, and looked eastward, with more of life than it had displayed for days. Thereafter it tried continually to turn aside. But Price, with merciless *mas'hab* stick, drove it on toward the mountain.

After a time he could make out men standing upon the high black walls. Tiny dolls in blue. Little more than moving blue specks. But he thought they were jeering at him, taunting him with Aysa's captivity, with their walled security upon the cliffs. He found himself cursing them, in a voice that was a whispering croak.

Then, again, when he was nearer the mountain, men rode to meet him. Men in hooded robes of blue, upon white racing-camels. Nine of them, armed with long, yellow-bladed pikes, and golden *yataghans*.

Price drove his staggering *hejin* on toward them, whispering insane curses. He knew that they were branded with the mark of the golden snake, that they were the human slaves of the golden man, of Malikar, who had stolen Aysa.

They stopped on the bare lava before him, and awaited his coming.

With a thin arm he lifted the golden ax that was slung to the pommel of his saddle. Trying in vain to goad his dromedary to a trot, he advanced, croaking out the syllables of the ax-song of Iru.

And abruptly the nine whirled, as if in consternation, before this gaunt, golden-armored warrior upon a reeling skeleton of a camel, and fled back toward the mountain, and around it.

Price's mount was still trying to turn off toward the right, but he followed on after the nine. They left him far behind, but at last he rounded the sheer shoulder of crystalline basalt, that leapt up in colossal hexagonal columns toward the bright castle, and came to the east side of the mountain.

The men were again in view, sitting still upon their camels and looking apprehensively back, when Price came around the mountain. They delayed a little longer, and then retreated again. They rode directly into the mountain.

Again Price followed. At the top of a short slope he saw a square black tunnel in the cliff, the opening of a horizontal shaft driven straight into the basalt.

He started up the lava slope. The *hejin* fell weakly to its knees, and refused to get up again. Price got out of the saddle, took the golden ax and the yellow oval shield, and started on afoot.

A heavy clang of metal reached his ears, and he saw that the mouth of the tunnel had vanished. In its place was a square of bright gold, inlaid in the black mountain wall.

It was madness. He knew that he had driven himself

122

harder than a man, by rights, can go. He knew that he could not longer trust his senses. Perhaps, after all, there had been no tunnel. The men who fled might have been figments of delirium.

But he reeled on up the slope, in the bright mail of Iru, with the ax and the buckler of the old king of Anz.

He came to the yellow square in the basaltic mountain's flank. His eyes had not deceived him; there had been a tunnel. Golden gates had closed it. He saw the seam down the middle, the massive hinges on either side. Broad panels of yellow gold, twenty feet high, smooth, polished so that he could see his reflection in them.

He paused an instant, wondering. Was this Price Durand? This thin, stern figure, with staring, sunken, glassy eyes. With black, swollen lips. With madness and death upon a wild and haggard face. Was Price Durand this gaunt specter in golden mail, carrying the arms of a king centuries dust?

The wonder at himself came and fled, like any idea of his desert-maddened brain—like any idea save the one that did not change, the single idea that he must find Aysa.

Then his croaking voice was demanding in Arabic that the golden doors be opened. He heard a subdued stirring beyond the panels, but they did not move.

He whispered the ax-song of Iru, and hammered upon the mocking golden valves with the battle-ax. And yet they did not open.

Still he beat upon the gates, and shrilled dry-voiced curses, and croaked Aysa's name. And shining silence taunted him.

Then the dominating purpose that had driven him through

terrible days was broken. His reason found sanctity in madness from suffering in a land too cruel for life. And Price was left the creature of delirium.

13. THE GOLDEN LAND

THROUGH several days Price drifted lazily back from temporary insanity into slow awareness. He was among Arabs. Arabs who dressed oddly, and spoke a curious archaic dialect. They were his friends, or rather, awe-struck worshippers. They called him Iru.

He recalled vaguely that somewhere he had heard this strange dialect before. He had even heard the name Iru. But it was several days before he remembered the circumstances of his hearing either.

He lay upon rugs and cushions in a long room, dark and cool, with smoothly plastered mud walls. A guard of the strange Arabs was always near him. And a man who seemed their leader had come many times to see him.

Yarmud was his name. A typical Arab, tall, thin-lipped, hawk-nosed. Price liked him. His dark eyes were straight and piercing. He carried himself with a simple, reserved dignity. Upon his lean, brown face was fierce, stern pride, almost regal.

Yarmud plainly was the ruler of these Arabs; yet he appeared to defer to Price as if to a greater potentate.

Price slept most of the time. He made no exertion save to drink the water and camel's milk, to eat the simple fare, that his hosts offered him where he lay. He did not try to question them, or even to think. The hardships of his terrible march upon the tiger's trail had brought him near death, indeed. Tortured body and fevered mind recovered but slowly.

Then one afternoon, when Yarmud entered the room, a

stately, august figure in his long, oddly fashioned black *abba*, Price awoke. His mind was suddenly sane and clear again. He rose to meet the old Arab, though his limbs felt yet weak.

Old Yarmud smiled flashingly in pleasure to see him rise.

"*Salaam aleikum,* Lord Iru," he called. And, to Price's astonishment, he dropped to his knees on the floor.

Price returned the immemorial desert formula, and Yarmud rose, anxiously inquiring about his health.

"Oh, I'm coming around all right," he assured the Arab. "How long have I been here?"

"Five days ago your camel—or the camel of the maiden Aysa, who went to wake you—came to the lake. You, Iru, were fastened upon the beast, with a halter-rope around your body and the pommels of the saddle."

He knew, then, that this must be the town of El Yerim, from which Aysa had fled. These people thought him the legendary king of Anz, awakened to free them from bondage to the golden beings. No great wonder that, since he had ridden out of the desert with the weapons of the ancient ruler, looking more dead than alive.

"The mountain where Malikar lives," he asked, "is it near?"

Yarmud gestured with a lean arm. "Northwest. The journey of half a day."

Price realized then that his *hejin*, when it tried to turn aside on the last day of the ride to the mountain, had been trying to come to the oasis here. He supposed that, after abandoning his insane hammering upon the golden gate, he had retained consciousness enough to mount the dromedary and tie himself to the saddle, though he recalled nothing of it. And the loyal animal had brought him here.

"Aysa?" he asked Yarmud, eagerly. "Know you where she is?"

"No. She was chosen by Malikar to go to the mountain with the snake's tribute. She escaped, none knew how," the old Arab glanced at Price, with the suggestion of a wink, "and went in search of Anz, the lost city, to waken you. You know not where she is?"

Price's heart went out to Yarmud, with the certainty that he had connived at Aysa's escape.

"No. Malikar came, and carried her off. He left me locked in the old catacombs. I got out and followed the tracks of his tiger. They led to the mountain."

"We shall free her," said Yarmud, "when we destroy the golden folk."

Noticing Price's weakness, the old ruler soon departed, leaving him to decide one problem that had risen. These Arabs obviously considered Price the miraculous resurrection of their ancient king. As such, they were no doubt ready to follow him in a war against the golden beings.

Since he had the old king's arms—mail, ax and shield were beside his bed—and since he knew the ax-song, it might be easy enough for him to play the part. But Price was naturally frank, straightforward. Everything in him revolted at assuming false colors.

Next morning he was feeling stronger. And he had made his decision.

When Yarmud entered again, and was about to kneel, Price stopped him. "Wait. You call me by the name of the king of lost Anz. But I am not Iru. My name is Price Durand."

Yarmud gaped at him.

"I was born in another land," Price explained. "I came here across the sea and the mountains."

The Arab recovered, remonstrated excitedly:

"But you must be Iru! You are tall: you have the blue eyes, the flaming hair! Aysa went to seek you, found you. You yourself say that you broke from the tomb. You come from Anz with the ax of Iru, and whispering his ax-song."

Price began an explanation of his life, and the expedition into the desert, of how he had come to meet Aysa.

"Yes, those strangers are here," Yarmud agreed. "They camp across the lake. They take our food, and turn their camels on our pasture, and give us no pay. They wish my warriors to march with them against the golden folk. But none of them is, like you, the image of Iru."

In the end, Price was unable to convince Yarmud that he was not the ancient king, returned. Like Aysa, the old man cheerfully admitted his story, but insisted that he was Iru, born again. And though he was unwilling to accept any theory, that he was the reincarnation of a barbarian king, Price could find no effective argument against it.

"Promise me that you will say no more that you are not Iru," at last Yarmud demanded, shrewdly, "for my warriors are eager to follow you against the golden folk."

And Price, for Aysa's sake, was glad enough to promise. After all, there might be something in Yarmud's contention. He did not intend to trouble himself further about it. The problems of one life were proving quite enough.

Aysa, Price found, was the daughter of Yarmud's brother, who had been sheikh of the Beni Anz, until Malikar had done away with him two harvest-seasons before, for refusal to send the annual tribute to the snake. Yarmud, then, his successor, was Aysa's uncle—which fact further increased Price's liking for the sternly proud old ruler.

Late that afternoon Price, for the first time, left the long room in which he had awakened.

"When Aysa escaped, Malikar demanded more tribute to the snake," Yarmud told him. "A camel laden with dates and grain, and another maiden. The snake-men have come today to take them."

Price expressed desire to watch the departure of the sacrifice.

"You may," Yarmud agreed. "But you should dress as one of my warriors. It would not be well for Malikar to know you are here, before we strike."

He arrayed Price in a long, flowing *gumbaz,* a brown *abba,* and a vivid green *kafiyeh,* which concealed his red hair; armed him with a long, two-edged bronze sword and a broad-bladed spear with a wooden shaft.

Mingling with a score of men similarly dressed, Price went out into El Yerim.

He found himself upon the dusty, irregular streets of a town half concealed in groves of date-palms. The clustered mud buildings, low and squat, were of the simple, massive adobe architecture old as Babylon. The streets were deserted save for groups of Arab warriors; an air of silent dread hung over them.

Then Price's eyes went to what the others were watching.

Two hundred yards from where Price and the Arab warriors stood, along the broad bare strip of gravel between the adobe town and the little lake, stood a dozen white camels. Blue-robed men, armed with shimmering yellow *yataghans*, sat upon five of them, holding the halter-ropes of the others. One was loaded with wicker hampers; that, he supposed, was part of the tribute.

A thin wailing shriek of agonized grief rose among the low mud houses. And the remaining six snake-men came into view, two of them dragging between them a young girl whose hands were lashed behind her. Behind followed a haggard woman, screaming and beating her flat breasts.

The girl seemed submissive, paralyzed with fear. She made no struggle as she was lifted to one of the mounted men, who laid her inert body across the saddle before him.

Hastening northward along the brown adobe walls, they came out of the town, upon the gravel shore of a tiny lake. Its crystal water was boiling up in the center, from the uprush of the great springs that fed it—and made possible this desert garden that Quadra y Vargas had called "the golden land."

Green-tufted palms lined the opposite shore, and under them Price saw the camp of the expedition with which he had come into the desert. The trim khaki drill tents of Jacob Garth and the other whites. The black camel's hair *hejras* of the sheik Fouad el Akmet and his Bedouins. The gray silent bulk of the army tank. Little groups of men were standing beneath the palms, watching; he recognized bulky Jacob Garth and Joao de Castro.

The other men leapt upon their camels, and wheeled them, almost running down the grief-stricken woman.

Price ran forward impulsively as the eleven started around the lake, one of them leading the laden camel. Yarmud gripped his arm, stopped him.

"Wait Iru," he whispered. "You are not yet strong from your ride. Nor are we ready for battle. If we interfere, Malikar will come and bathe El Yerim in blood. And Vekyra—she will hunt the human game! Wait, until we are ready."

Price stopped, realizing the wisdom of the sheikh's words. But hot rage filled him, the burning resentment he always felt when he saw the weak abused by the strong. And cold determination filled him to destroy utterly the golden beings—be they human or living metal—that had subjected this race to such base slavery. Before, he might have been satisfied with the rescue of Aysa. Now he was filled with a stern and passionless resolve to obliterate the beings who had taken her from him.

14. THE MENACE IN THE MIRAGE

THE Price Durand who rode around the little lake, five days later, and into the *farengi* camp, with Yarmud and twoscore warriors of the Beni Anz, was not the same restless wanderer, who had set out with the expedition from the Arabian Sea, so many weary weeks before.

He felt completely recovered, now, from the suffering of his last cruel journey, and filled with a burning impatience to test his strength with Malikar that would brook no longer delay.

The desert sun had burned him to the brown of an Arab, had drawn every superfluous drop of moisture from his body. He was hard, lean, wiry. A new iron strength was in him, bred of the desert he had fought and mastered.

His spirit was hardened as much as his supple body. He had joined Jacob Garth, not in quest of gold, but a restless malcontent, a weary sportsman in search of a new game, a world-rover driven by vague and obscure longings.

In the Rub Al Khali he had found Aysa, strange lovely girl, fugitive from weird peril. He had fled with her across the shifting sands . . . loved her in the hidden garden of a lost city . . . lost her to a power that he did not yet understand.

Now he was determined to find and free the girl, to blot out the beings that had taken her. It was as if the desert life had crystallized all his restless energy into a single driving power that would yield to no opposition, admit no failure.

He knew that very real and immediate danger faced the attempt. The powers of the golden beings, as he had

132

glimpsed them, were vast and ominous, appalling. But it was not in Price to consider the consequences of defeat, save as challenge to another battle.

Jacob Garth came out of his tent, to meet Price and his bodyguard. Always an enigma, the huge man was unchanged. His puffy, tallow-white face was blandly placid, mask-like, as ever; pale, cold blue eyes still peered blankly and unfeelingly from above his tangle of curly red beard.

He stopped, and surveyed Price for a time, and then his voice rang out, richly sonorous, in casual greeting, free from hint of surprize:

"Hello, Durand."

"Good morning, Garth."

Price looked down from his *hejin*—Yarmud's gift—at the gross, bovinely calm man in dusty khaki. He felt the cold eyes taking in his gleaming chain mail, his bright shield, the yellow ax.

"Where've you been, Durand?" Garth boomed suddenly.

Price met his searching, unreadable gaze. "We've a good deal to talk over, Garth. Suppose we adjourn somewhere out of the sun?"

"Will you come in my tent, over here under the palms?"

Price nodded. He dismounted and gave the halter-rope of his camel to one of Yarmud's men. With a word to the old sheikh, he followed Jacob Garth to the tent, entered before him. Garth motioned to a blanket spread on the gravel floor; they squatted on it.

The big man stared at him, silently, rather grimly, then spoke suddenly:

"You understand, Durand, that you aren't returning to

133

your old place as leader of this expedition. I don't know just how the men will want to dispose of you, since your—desertion."

"That affair was revolt against my authority!" cried Price. "And against every law of human decency. I'm no deserter!" He caught himself. "But we needn't go into that. And your men won't be called upon to dispose of me."

"You appear to be in cahoots with the natives," Garth observed.

"They have accepted me as a leader. We are planning an attack on the mountain of the golden folk. I came to see if you would care to join the expedition."

Jacob Garth seemed more interested. "They will actually follow you?" he demanded. "Against their golden gods?"

"I think so."

"Then perhaps we can come to some agreement." The deep voice was suave as ever, colorless. "We've been here for weeks. The men are rested, ready for action. We've been drilling. And scouting over the country.

"We'd have moved on the mountain already, but the natives refused to join me. And it appeared bad strategy to advance and leave them in control of the water. We didn't trust them."

"I'm sure," Price said, "of the entire loyalty of the Beni Anz—or at least of Yarmud, the sheikh—to me. I propose that we join forces—until the golden people are smashed."

"And then?"

"You and the men can help yourselves to the golden palace. All I want is Aysa's safety."

"You mean the woman you took away from de Castro?"

Price nodded.

"Well, Joao is going to have something to say about her. I promised him his choice of any women we take. But, for my part, I accept your terms."

"We're allies, then?"

"Until we have broken the power of the golden folk."

Jacob Garth extended his puffy hand. Price took it, and was amazed again at the crushing strength beneath the smooth soft skin.

At sunrise the next morning a veritable army was winding through the palm groves of El Yerim, from the camp and the town beside the tiny lake. The clattering tank led the van. Behind rode men on camels, in a close, double column.

Jacob Garth and sloe-eyed Joao de Castro, at the head of the *farengi,* a score of hard-bitten adventurers, their pack animals laden with machine-guns, the mountain artillery. Stokes mortars, and high explosives.

The sheikh Fouad el Akmet riding before his two-score *nakhawilah,* who were proudly girt with glittering cartridge belts and carrying new Lebel rifles.

Price Durand, resplendent in the golden mail of Iru, riding beside Yarmud at the head of nearly five hundred eager warriors of the Beni Anz.

As the interminable line of fighting-men crept out of the green palm groves of the fertile valley, to the desolate, fire-born plateau, they came in view of *Hajar Jehannum,* or Verl, as the Beni Anz named the mountain—a steep-walled, basaltic butte, the core of an ancient volcano, crowned with a towered palace ablaze with myriad splintering gleams of white and gold.

An exultant cheer rolled back along the columns, as each successive group came within view of the mountain, with the bright promise of its coronal of marble and yellow metal.

Price's heart lifted. Involuntarily he urged his *hejin* to a faster gait, fondled the oaken helve of Korlu, the great ax. Aysa must be a prisoner within that scintillating castle. Aysa, the fair, brave girl of the desert.

"Great is the day!" Yarmud shouted beside him, kicking his own camel to make it keep pace. "Before sunset the castle of Verl is ours. At last the golden folk shall die——"

Fear stilled his voice. Silently, pale-faced, he pointed at the bleak mountain still fifteen miles away. The whole long column had abruptly halted; a dry whisper of terror raced along it.

"The shadow of the golden folk!" came Yarmud's fear-roughened voice.

A brilliant fan of light was lifting into the indigo sky ahead. Narrow rays of rose and topaz mingled in an inverted, splendid pyramid of flame. The apex of the pyramid touched the highest golden tower. The colored rays were up-flung from the castle.

Above the fan of saffron and rosy glory a picture appeared. Vague at first, looming gigantic as if projected on the dome of the blue heavens, it swiftly took form, color, reality.

136

A gigantic snake, vast as a cloud, coiled in the air above the mountain. A heap of yellow coils, the evil head uplifted upon a slender gleaming aureate column. A serpent of gold. Each brilliant scale glinted like polished metal. The head dropped upon the upmost coil, and the snake's eyes, glittering black, insidious, looked down upon the halted columns.

Beside the serpent was a woman—the same woman, Price knew, that he had seen upon the tiger, in the mirage above the mountain pass. A yellow coil, thick as her body, was looped about her feet, and she half reclined against the next, an arm caressingly over it.

The woman's body was yellow as the snake, and she had something of the serpent's slender, sinuous grace. A short, tight-fitting tunic of green encased it, hiding no undulating line. Red-golden, flowing loose and abundant, her hair fell over her yellow shoulders.

The woman looked down from the sky, a mockingly malefic smile upon her oval, exotic face. Her full lips, crimsoned, were voluptuous and cruel; the lids of her piquantly slanted eyes dark-edged; the shadowed orbs themselves tawny-green.

Price watched those greenish, oblique eyes rove the columns, questingly, and fasten suddenly upon himself. The woman, apparently, saw him as plainly as he did her, whatever the strange agency of her projection. She stared down at him, boldly. In her gaze was a curious intimacy.

Then puzzlement and vague alarm came into the tawny eyes, as they absorbed the golden mail, the oval buckler, the yellow ax. But still they held a taunting challenge, an

137

enigmatic promise, too, oddly disturbing. The slim yellow body relaxed against the thick, heaped golden coils of the snake. Reddened fingers shook out the ruddy-golden hair until it rippled in shimmering cascades.

Price was swept with a surge of fierce desire for that full-curved, sinuous body. He felt swift will to meet the taunting mockery in the greenish, slanted eyes. Lust, not love. Nothing of the spirit, nothing reverent.

He laughed at the woman, derisively. She flung back the silken-gold net of hair, abruptly, and anger flashed in the tawny eyes. No doubt that she saw him.

He looked away from her, at the snake. Even by comparison with the looming shadow of the woman it was large, its golden-scaled body thicker than her own. Like an ominous cloud, it hung in the sky above the black mountain, above the outspread fan of arrowed rays. Flat, triangular, ugly, its great head watched.

Its glittering eyes were terrible; black with a hint of purple, unwinking, aflame with cold light. Price's pulse slowed with instinctive fear as he met them, icy needles danced along his spine. The eyes of the snake were wells of cold evil, agleam with sinister wisdom older than mankind. They were hypnotic.

Price had wondered how a rabbit feels, frozen in fascinated trance, as the stalking snake writhes near. In that moment he knew. He felt the cold, deadly shock of resistless, malign *power*, intangible, inexplicable, yet terrifyingly real.

With an effort he dragged his gaze away from those motionless, hypnotic orbs. His body, to his surprise, was tense, covered with chill sweat.

Looking back along the columns, he saw that a strange quietness had fallen, a silence almost of death. Every man was gazing fascinated into the mirage. Clatter of voices was stilled. No outcry rose, even of wonder or fear.

"Attention!" he shouted. Then, in Arabic: "Don't look at the snake. Turn away. Look back toward the oasis. The snake has no power unless you watch it."

A deep sigh beside him. And Yarmud's low voice:

"The snake threatens. We will win no easy victory. Its eyes can destroy us."

"Let's go on." Price urged his camel forward.

"Then sing the ax-song. The men are afraid."

Price lifted his voice in the battle-song of the ancient barbarian king whose armor he wore. A wave of cheering rolled back along the column, at first feeble and uncertain, but rising in volume.

And the long line crept forward again.

15. MIRRORS OF PERIL

AS THE hours went by and the camel-mounted columns wound onward, the weird mirage hung ominously in the sky ahead, tawny-green eyes of the golden woman and purple-black orbs of the snake gazing down. At times the phenomenon appeared curiously near. It seemed to draw steadily away, as the expedition advanced, keeping a uniform distance.

Price speculated upon possible scientific explanations of it, without arriving at any satisfactory conclusion. The mirage, he knew, must be simply the colossal reflection of real beings, produced by the application of optical laws unknown to the outside world.

The hypnotic or paralytic effect of the snake's eyes was even more puzzling. He supposed that the golden reptile merely possessed the slight power of fascination of the ordinary snake, increased in proportion to its size, and perhaps intensified or amplified in the same manner as its body was magnified in the mirage.

The men remained subdued and frightened. The courage of Fouad and his Bedouins was maintained only by their confidence in the tank and the other invincible weapons of the *farengi* band. The Beni Anz were similarly sustained by a faith in Price as a supernatural deliverer.

Many times the column lagged. Price and Jacob Garth and Yarmud rode continually back and forth, encouraging the men, warning them not to look into the maddening mirage hanging ahead, where the snake's eyes gleamed

140

with the cold and deadly fascination of ancient and sinister wisdom.

As they drew near the mountain, Price sent out scouts.

Five miles from the black, basaltic mass, the head of the column reached the edge of a shallow *wadi*, a valley a thousand yards across. Three scouts, upon fleet *hejins*, were half across its level floor, when the low black lava-crowned hills above the opposite slope burst into menacing life.

Scores of blue-clad men appeared from nowhere, dragging to the hill-crest great, silvery, ellipsoid mirrors that flickered in the sun; mirrors supported upon metal frames, like the one that had slain the Arab Hamed with an invisible ray of cold, in the mountain pass.

Broad bright ellipsoids wavered and shimmered in the sun. Queer flashes of violet darted from them, strangely painful to the eye.

At first appearance of the enemy, the three scouts turned and dashed madly back, but not swiftly enough to escape the mirrors. The camel in the lead stumbled and fell. Rider and mount shattered, splintered, when they struck the ground, bodies suddenly chilled to the point of brittleness. The fragments quickly were silvered with frost.

An instant later the second man went down, in a swirl of snow-flakes. Then the third, with a crash like breaking glass.

Fear swept the column on the low lava hills above the *wadi*. The brooding menace of the mirage had been endurable because it was distant, half unreal. These mirrors of cold were as terrifyingly strange, as they were immediately dangerous. Bedouins and Beni Anz stirred uneasily, but at sight of Price and Jacob Garth unmoved ahead of them, held their ground.

Defense was swiftly organized. Garth boomed rapid orders. The Krupp mountain guns, the four Hotchkiss machine-guns, the two Stokes mortars, were quickly unpacked, mounted in covered positions along the hilltop.

The sheikh Fouad El Akmet's men were gathered behind the tank to follow it in the first charge. The four hundred and eighty warriors of the Beni Anz, armed, save for a hundred archers, only with long swords and spears, were held for the moment in reserve, in the rear.

The two little cannons were soon thudding regularly, sweeping the opposite slope of the *wadi* with screaming shrapnel. The Hotchkiss guns broke into rattling music, and snipers, flung prone, nursed barking rifles.

A few minutes longer the mirrors flashed with eye-searing violet. Little swirls of frost appeared in the air about the gunners, and several men fell, shivering, temporarily paralyzed. But the range was apparently too great for effective use of the mirrors. They were dragged back beyond the lava ridge, out of view again.

Price and Jacob Garth, near the guns, scanned the opposite side of the *wadi* through binoculars. A dozen still blue forms were sprawled there, victims of bullets and shrapnel splinters. But the living had vanished.

"Our move," Garth observed, serenely bland as ever.

"Can't afford to leave the initiative up to them. And the ammunition for the Krupps won't hold out all day."

He turned to boom orders.

The gray-armored tank lumbered over the crest of the hill. At top speed it rumbled down the slope and clanked across the *wadi's* stony floor, machine-guns hammering. Behind it raced Fouad's Bedouins, with their new Lebel rifles.

In undisciplined but splendid charge the Arabs dashed after the tank, throwing up their rifles to fire in headlong career. They were half-way across the valley when the mirrors of cold were pushed back to the hill before them.

One Arab fell with his camel into a frosty heap of shattered fragments. Another, then two more, went down in clouds of glittering ice. Then the tank was abruptly white, gleaming argent.

A few seconds it lumbered on. Price hoped that its armor had been proof against the ray; remembered how nearly he had been frozen in it, back in the Jebel Harb. The roaring motor faltered, died. The tank veered, turned broadside to the enemy, stood silent and motionless, a silvery ghost of itself. He felt quick regret for old Sam Sorrows.

Though the Krupps and machine-guns were still raining death upon the blue-clad crews of the mirrors, the tank's failure shattered the morale of the Arabs. Wheeling their racing dromedaries, they plunged back in mad retreat. And two more fell as they fled.

Disaster was unpleasantly near, Price realized. The

143

proudest weapon of the *farengi* had fallen a quick victim to the mirrors of cold. Another such reverse would set the Arabs in panic flight.

"Want to try a charge with your natives, Durand?" asked Garth. "That's about the only chance. We'll be helpless when the ammunition's gone."

Price looked across the *wadi* with narrowed eyes. It would cost many lives to gain the opposite hill; but, if they retreated now, the Beni Anz would never find courage to advance again.

"All right," he told Garth.

"Good luck. I'll keep up the fire." The big man took his hand in that puffy paw that was so surprizingly strong.

Five minutes later Price rode down into the *wadi*, swinging the golden ax and raising his voice in the barbaric chant of Iru. Behind his racing *hejin* came the Beni Anz warriors, in long, irregular lines and scattered groups, scattered purposely.

Half a mile ahead was the low, lava-crowned hill, glittering with half a score of huge, spinning mirrors. Blue-robed men crowded about them, many falling beneath Garth's fire, but others springing from the hidden trenches to replace them.

Camel's feet beat upon the stony ground with a vast, hollow thunder. Eager, exultant cries rang out, repeated phrases of the ax-song: "Kill . . . Korlu the red doom . . . Drinker of life-blood . . . Keeper of death-gate."

Ellipsoid mirrors swayed and spun, flashed painfully violet.

Price did not look back. Shouting the ax-song, he

charged straight on; but he heard the screams of terror, and sharp, splintering crashes, like the shattering of myriad panes of glass—the sound of frozen men and camels, smashing to fragments on the rocks.

A blast of icy air struck his face, misty with floating ice-crystals—breath-taking. A freezing ray had come perilously near.

He rode on. The wild drumming of feet behind did not falter.

At last Price's dromedary was leaping up the hill, toward the nearest mirror. The broad, shimmering ellipsoid swung toward him—a six-foot sheet of silvery metal, mounted upon a delicate, elaborate mechanism.

Two blue-robes were behind it, the glittering brand of the snake upon their foreheads. As one turned the mirror, another manipulated a little knob.

Price saw a violet glow flush the argent metal.

Then he had leapt his camel upon the machine. It collapsed, with a rending and crashing of metal. The *hejin* fell sprawling. Price sprang clear of the saddle, plunged for the two blue-robes with the great ax.

It took place with the disordered swiftness of a dream.

One moment, a dozen blue-clad snake-men were surrounding Price, with wicked, double-curved yellow *yataghans*. The next, the charging Beni Anz were rolling about him like a resistless wave.

Fire from Krupps and machine-guns had ceased as they neared the ridge. And the mirrors of cold ceased to function as their crews were ridden down by camel-mounted warriors.

Savage battle raged for a few minutes along the hilltop, with no quarter given. Two hundred of the Beni Anz had fallen upon the *wadi* floor, but those who survived to reach the hill exacted a terrible price for their fallen comrades.

A little time of utter confusion. Blue snake-men rallying about their mirrors. Camels crashing through them, kicking, slashing with yellow tusks. Men and camels falling, before arrow and *yataghan* and spear.

Price, on foot, held his own. The great ax drank blood, and the barbaric song of Iru still rang out.

Then, abruptly, amazingly, the battle was won.

Along the crest of the hill stood the great mirrors, twisted, wrecked. Around them, and in the shallow, lava-walled trenches behind them, lay motionless, gory blue-clad bodies—the snake-men were down, to the last man. Here and there were camels, dead or dying. The survivors of the Beni Anz, no more than half the number that had begun the charge, were swiftly stripping the dead, loading camels with their loot.

Behind lay the grim black *wadi* floor, scattered with white, shattered heaps that had been men and camels, the silvery, silent tank among them.

Price looked toward the mountain.

Five miles away across the bleak, dark desolation of the lava fields rose its forbidding basaltic masses; cyclopean black pillars and columns, soaring up two thousand feet, to the glittering splendor of snowy marble and burnished gold that was the palace of the yellow people.

From the dome of the highest gorgeous tower yet spread the fan of lanced rays of rose and topaz light. Above the rays, the weird mirage still hung. Braving the serpent's hypnotic eyes, Price ventured another glance at it.

The yellow woman, still beside the giant snake, still caressing it, met his glance with a mocking, derisive smile, and shrugged her slim yellow shoulders, as much as to say: "Perhaps you have won, but what of it?"

"Malikar!" wailed one of the Arabs in sudden terror. "Malikar comes! On the golden tiger!"

Dropping his eyes from the mirage, Price saw the yellow tiger running across the lava plain from the mountain. A gigantic beast, fully the size of an ordinary elephant, it carried the ebon *howdah*, with Malikar, the golden man, seated in it.

Still several miles away, the giant cat was covering distance at a surprizing rate. Obviously terrified, the Beni Anz warriors frantically loaded the last of their plunder, and began leading their camels back into the *wadi*.

149

16. THE STRANGE EYES OF THE SNAKE

IT WAS now high noon. Merciless white sun-flame drove down upon the lifeless volcanic plain beyond the ridge, across which the yellow tiger was running, and beat upon the rugged lava slopes below the towering cone of *Hajar Jehannum.* No wind stirred; the air trembled with stinging heat.

After a few moments' thought, Price decided to retire into the *wadi* he had just crossed at such expense in human lives, to await Malikar's coming. He did not like to retreat before a single man. But he was not sure that Malikar was a man; he wanted to get beneath the cover of Jacob Garth's guns.

Midway across the stony floor, where the grisly piles of white were now turning red, he stopped the Arabs, waited, dispatching a note to Jacob Garth to inform him of the victory on the hill and warn him of Malikar's coming.

Very soon the yellow tiger appeared upon the hill, among the wrecked mirrors of cold and the bodies of the blue-robed dead. For a time the gigantic beast stood there, Malikar sitting in the *howdah,* robed in red, staring about him.

Then the Krupp guns began to fire again. Price heard the whine of shrapnel above his head. And he saw white smoke burst up near the motionless tiger, where high explosive shells were falling.

Then a strange thing happened.

Malikar stood up in the *howdah,* turned back to face the mirage still hanging in the sky above the black mountain. He flung out his arms in a gesture of command.

150

The yellow woman turned, and appeared to speak to the snake.

Gigantic, incredible, bright scales glittering metallic, xanthic yellow, the great serpent moved in the sky. The broad flat wedge of its head was lifted high, upon the slender, shining gold column of its neck. To and fro it swayed, slowly, regularly, purple-black eyes hypnotically a-glitter.

Price tried to draw his eyes away from the snake—and could not! Strange and coldly evil, those swaying, hypnotic orbs riveted him with baleful fascination. His whole body was paralyzed. He could scarcely breathe. A throbbing oppression was in his head; his throat was dry, constricted; his limbs were cold.

Sounds of firing ceased, from the guns across the *wadi;* Price knew that the others had also been seized by this incredible paralysis.

Brilliant purple-black, the serpent's eyes shone with cold force of utter evil. Dark wisdom filled them—wisdom older than the race of man. Overwhelming, resistless *will.*

Price began a battle to move. Deadly paralysis claimed him. A dull weight rested on his brain; his head swam. Suffocation choked him. Coldness crept up his limbs, prickling deadness.

But he was not going to surrender. He wasn't going to let himself be hypnotized by a snake. Not even a golden snake, in a mirage of madness. A matter of wills. He would *not* be mastered!

His head was turning, involuntarily, to follow the swaying serpent's orbs. He tensed the muscles of his neck, struggled to keep his head motionless, to turn his eyes downward.

151

Then his whole body tensed. He had the incredible sensation that the snake realized his resistance, was increasing the hypnotic power that chained him. Price set his jaw, jerked his head down.

All his will went into the effort. And a cord of evil seemed to snap. He was free. Weak, trembling, with a feeling of nausea in the pit of his stomach, but free! He dared himself to look back at the snake's eyes. And the dread paralysis did not return. He had proved his mastery.

Price turned, reeling uncertainly. He saw a sickening thing.

Standing about him were two-score Beni Anz warriors, afoot, as he was. All were frozen in rigid paralysis, staring up into the mirage. Mute, helpless terror was on their white, sweat-beaded faces. Their eyes were glazed, they breathed slowly, gaspingly. And Malikar was murdering them.

The gold giant had dismounted from the yellow tiger, which stood two-score yards away. Swiftly he was passing from one to another of the motionless, paralyzed men, methodically stabbing each in the breast with a long, two-edged sword.

The men stood in tense paralysis, staring at the fatal mirage, heads turning a little to follow the swaying, hypnotic eyes of the snake. Helpless, naked horror was on their faces; they were unaware of Malikar, so near.

The yellow man worked swiftly, driving his blade with dexterous skill into unguarded breasts, withdrawing it with a jerk as he pushed his victims backward, to sprawl with red blood welling out.

Outraged, half sick with the brutal horror of it, Price shouted something, sprang toward him.

Malikar turned suddenly, his red robe dripping with new blood. A moment he was startled, motionless, with fear unmistakable in his shallow, tawny eyes. Then he leapt to meet Price, brandishing his reeking blade.

Price met the sword-thrust with the golden buckler, and swung the ax. The yellow man sprang back; but the ax-blade grazed his shoulder, the bloody sword clattered from his fingers.

Price ran forward over the rocky ground, to follow up his advantage. Luck was against him. A loose stone turned under his foot; he stumbled, went heavily to his knees.

As he staggered back to his feet, Malikar leapt away, picked up a heavy block of lava, flung it at him. Price tried in vain to dodge. He felt the impact of the missile against his head; crimson flame seemed to burst from it, flaring through all his brain.

When Price groaned and sat up it was just past sunset. The cool wind that had roused him was blowing down from the black mass of the mountain across the bleak lava flows northward. In the fading, rosy light the gold-and-white palace above the frowning walls was a splendorous coronal. And the mirage was gone.

Price woke where Malikar had felled him. The *wadi's* stony floor was red with piles of thawed flesh and shattered bone. Near him were the score of men Malikar had stabbed as they were helpless in that dread fascination of the snake, white *kafiyehs* scarlet-stained.

He was alone with the dead. Malikar was gone, with the

tiger. And the Beni Anz, and Fouad's men, and Jacob Garth's. But the little tank still stood there, where the ray of cold had stopped it, in the middle of the *wadi*.

With a dull and heavy sense of despair, Price realized that once again Malikar had defeated him. Bitterly he recalled the stone that had turned under his foot. The Durand luck had failed again.

His allies must have retreated in mad haste; perhaps they had broken the spell of the mirage, even as he had done, and fled. The abandonment of the tank, of himself and the possessions of the men about him, was proof enough of flight.

Not again, after this reverse, would the Beni Anz follow him, he knew. "Iru" would be discredited. And Aysa— lovely Aysa of the many moods, serious and smiling, de- mure and gay, strange, daring fugitive of the sand-waste— was still locked in the mountain fortress ahead, more than ever hopelessly lost.

A missile flicked past Price's head and clattered startlingly on the bare lava. He heard the clatter of running feet, a hoarse shout of rage and hate. Still dazed, stiff of move- ment, Price staggered to his feet, turned to face the assailant who had crept up behind him in the twilight.

Wicked yellow *yataghan* upraised, the man was charging at him in the dusk, a dozen yards away. A tall Arab in a queerly hooded robe of blue. He must, like Price, be a sur- vivor of the battle. He limped as he ran, or hopped grotesquely. And one side of his face was red horror, from which a wild eye, miraculously unharmed, glared with fanatic hate. On his high forehead was the gleaming yellow brand of a coiled serpent.

154

17. THE SLAVE OF THE SERPENT

AS PRICE DURAND stumbled to his feet, the world tilted and spun beneath him. His head drummed with pain. He reeled, and fought to keep his balance, while the stony *wadi* floor, strewn with the dead, whirled around him.

The basaltic mass of *Hajar Jehannum*, its golden-and-marble crown sullen in the red sunset, was first on one hand, then on the other. A wave of blackness rose about him, receded. Then the rocking desert steadied.

For a moment Price lost his attacker. Then he saw the Arab again, limping fiercely forward, whirling the *yataghan*. One leg half dragging, he came with a series of bounding hops. Half his face was a scarlet, grinning smear; in his eyes was the lust of the killer.

Price fought to master his dizziness, and staggered backward to gain time. The heavy golden ax lay on the ground behind him, but he had neither time to reach it, nor strength, at the moment, to wield it.

He stumbled on the rough lava, swayed, regaining his balance with difficulty. But a measure of his strength was returning.

In a flash the snake-man was upon him, silent, breathing with quick, hot gasps like a struggling animal, driven by savage, fanatic hate. The double-curved *yataghan* swung up, and Price darted forward beneath it, one hand rushing for the Arab's sword-arm.

The mad rush of the wounded man flung them together. Despite Price's guarding arm, the yellow blade came against his side, rasping upon the linked golden mail he wore.

155

Then his arms were around the snake-man, and they toppled together to the stony ground.

With demoniacal energy the Arab tried to tear himself free, to use his wicked blade. Price clung desperately to his hold, biting his lip to keep back dizziness.

Suffering only from concussion and exhaustion, his muscles stiffened from his long period of unconsciousness, Price was recovering his strength with activity. And the snake-man, having lost much blood, animated merely by blind, mad hatred, rapidly collapsed.

His struggles weakened; suddenly he relaxed in Price's arms, unconscious. The wound in his thigh was bleeding, opened again by his struggles.

Appropriating the *yataghan*, Price moved a little away and stood, breathing hard, warily watching the snake-man.

"Mr. Durand?" Price started as the interrogative voice spoke unexpectely behind him. He whirled to see the lank Kansan, Sam Sorrows, staggering up behind him, arms laden.

"Why, Sam!" he ejaculated.

"Thought it must be you, Mr. Durand, in that golden coat. I didn't know there was anybody else alive around here."

"I didn't either, Sam. But there were three of us."

"Three?"

Price pointed to the unconscious Arab.

"Tie him up," the Kansan said, "and come on over to the tank. I've some loot here, for supper." He nodded at the bundles in his arms.

Price bound the snake-man's wrists and ankles with

kafiyehs taken from the dead Beni Anz warriors, roughly bandaged his bleeding thigh-wound, which was shallow and not serious, and followed Sam Sorrows to the side of the tank, where the old man was unloading his burden— small sacks of dried dates, coarse flour, and dried, powdered camel-flesh; and a full water-skin.

"Found these up in the trenches." He nodded across the *wadi*.

Squatting by the gray metal bulk looming in the dusk, they ate and drank.

"The mirrors got you, in the tank?" Price said after a time.

"Yes. Mawson was with me. The limey. He's dead. I was down driving. Guess I was better protected. But I must have been out quite a while.

"I was pretty sick when I came to. Cold as hell, shivering all over. And Mawson there, already stiff. I started to crawl out in the sunshine.

"I got my head out the manhole, and saw a lot of Arabs around the tank. Everything was quiet. All were looking up in the mirage, at that damned snake. The thing was swaying back and forth. Had them all charmed. I didn't more than glance at it, believe me!

"Then I saw the old tiger, standing there, big as an elephant, with the saddle on him. And a yellow man, down in front of him, stabbing those fellows that were looking in the mirage.

"Then you went at the yellow feller, and he knocked you out with a rock.

"About that time, I guess, some of the others were coming out of that damned spell. I heard the cannon go off a time or two, and shrapnel screaming over. The yellow man ran for his tiger again, and the Arabs broke and beat it. About that time I went under again."

"Jacob Garth?" demanded Price. "He got away?"

"I think so. Looked like they were packing up the guns when I went out again. Guess they'd had enough."

"What are you planning to do?"

"I was feeling pretty much knocked out when I came around again, an hour or so ago." The old man laughed a little. "Went out to see about rations. Thought I'd sleep aboard tonight, and try running back to the oasis in the morning. That okay with you? We ought to make it by noon."

Price merely nodded. He was thinking.

Returning to his captive an hour later, Price found the snake-man conscious again. After a moment's effort against his bonds, he lay quiet, glaring up at Price with hate-filled eyes.

"Who are you?" Price asked, in the archaic Arabic of the Beni Anz.

He did not answer, but the stubborn movement of his head, in the moonlight, told Price that he had understood.

Price returned to the tank, where Sam Sorrows was tinkering with his motor in anticipation of an early start, and brought back a canteen half full of water. He sloshed it noisily beside the man and repeated the question.

After half an hour, the Arab moved, and a voice spoke from the red ruin of his face:

"I am Kreor, a slave of the snake, under Malikar, priest of the snake."

And he whimpered for the water.

"No," Price told him. "You must tell me more, and promise to help me, if you would drink again."

"I am sworn to the snake," the man hissed. "And you are Iru, the ancient enemy of the snake and of Malikar. The eyes of the snake will seek me out and slay me, if I betray it."

"I'll see you are *dakhile*," Price assured him. "Forget the snake, if you would drink and serve me."

A long time the Arab was silent, staring scornfully up into the moon-swept sky. Price felt a surge of pity for him. He was near abandonment of his plan, when the snake-man whispered.

"So be it. I renounce the snake, and the service of Malikar under the snake. I am your slave, Iru. And *dakhile?*"

"*Dakhile,*" Price assured him again. But the voice of the Arab had a ring of duplicity that he did not like. He wished that the moonlight were brighter, so that he could see the man's face.

"Now give me water, Lord Iru."

Price thrust back his feelings again.

"First you must prove yourself. Answer me this question: Where is the girl named Aysa, whom Malikar brought from Anz?"

The snake-man hesitated, spoke reluctantly: "Aysa sleeps in the mists of gold, in the serpent's lair."

"What's that? Where is the serpent's lair?"

"Under the mountain. In the temple above the abyss of the mists of gold."

"Asleep, you say. What does that mean?" Panic edged his voice. "You don't mean she's dead?"

159

"No. She sleeps the long sleep of the golden vapor. Malikar honors her. She becomes one of the golden folk."

"Better explain this a little," Price said, menacingly. "Tell a straight story, if you want to drink again. What's this about golden mist?"

Again the Arab hesitated, glaring at him with crafty eyes in which hate was not wholly dead. Price sloshed the canteen; the other yielded.

"In the caverns beneath the mountain rises the vapor of gold, the breath of life. They who breathe it sleep. And sleeping, they become golden, as Malikar is golden, and deathless."

"Aysa, then, is being turned into gold?" Price inquired, incredulous.

"Yes. Soon her blood will be golden. When she wakes she will be priestess of the snake. And Vekyra indeed is wroth to know that Malikar has tired of *her*."

"Vekyra?" Price queried. "Who's she?"

"She is the old priestess of the snake. A woman of gold. Priestess—and Malikar's mistress."

"She's the one we saw in the mirage, over the mountain."

"In the sky? Yes. She is mistress also of the shadow. Vekyra has power of her own. Malikar will not easily be rid of her."

Price did not trust the man. Truth was hardly to be expected from a bound, helpless prisoner, who had been at one's throat an hour before. Moreover, thinly veiled hatred and scorn crept again and again into his voice. But, obviously, the Arab did not want to die. Some aid, some true information might be got from him. It would be a game of wits between them.

Was Aysa actually being turned into another monster of gold, by some diabolical chemical? It might easily be a fantastic lie on the snake-man's part. But the tale had a certain grim plausibility that edged Price's nerves with alarm.

"Do you know any way," Price demanded, "that we could get secretly into the mountain? To where Aysa is? Is that tunnel always guarded?"

Kreor lay silent again; he trembled.

"Answer me!" Price demanded. "Tell me if you can lead me to where the girl is?"

"The wrath of the snake, and Malikar," the Arab muttered.

"Remember, you are *dakhile.*"

"But I am wounded," the snake-man protested. "I could never reach the mountain."

"Your wounds aren't serious," Price assured him. "You can walk tomorrow, though perhaps a bit painfully. Speak."

"You could never get past the gates. They are always locked, and guarded."

"Is there another way?"

Again the man hesitated, and squirmed on the ground.

"Another way there is, Lord Iru. But perilous indeed."

"What is it?"

"High on the north wall of the mountain is a crevice. It leads into a great cave. From the cave is a way into the passages that lead down into the golden mist. But great is the peril, Iru. The climb is not easy; above the place of the snake are guards."

"We are going there," Price told him levelly, "as soon as you can walk. And unlucky it will be for you if you haven't told the truth."

He let the man drink. Bringing food from the tank, he

161

loosened his hands, so that he could eat, then bound him again.

Price and Sam Sorrows slept and watched by turns that night. As Price sat, leaning against the tank through the long hours of his watch, with the keen desert air about him and the cool stars looking down, he thought a great deal about the course of his adventures in this lost world, about what he should do on the morrow.

In the morning he could ride back to El Yerim in the tank, and the adventure would be over. The Beni Anz, he was certain, would not be willing to fight again under his leadership; old Yarmud would be remembering that he had denied being Iru. And he could hardly join Jacob Garth's party again, Joao de Castro hating him as he did.

If he turned back, there would be nothing to do save procure a camel, and strike out for civilization. He could never solve the weird riddles that had confronted him: the mystery of the mirage, of the golden folk. Infinitely worse, he would never see Aysa again.

On the other hand, he could remain with Kreor until the man recovered, and assault the mountain alone. It was a desperate plan. The Arab obviously hated him, would certainly betray him if opportunity presented. And opportunity was almost certain to appear.

The chance that he should ever leave the mountain alive appeared extremely slight. None the less, Price never really hesitated. The decision was inevitable.

"Back at camp by noon," Sam Sorrows predicted genially, as they breakfasted in the dawn.

"I'm not going with you," Price told him.

"What!"

"I'm going to try for the mountain on my own. Going to make that bird in the blue clothes guide me in. We'll hide around here until he can walk."

"But, Mr. Durand," the old man cried, "I—I don't like to see you try it, sir. I wouldn't trust that fellow. He's a—a snake!"

"I don't trust him. But he's the only shot."

Sam Sorrows stared at him, grinned and rose and shook his hand.

"Luck, Mr. Durand. A crazy thing to do, sir. But you might make it. I'll leave you the water-skin, and the grub. And you might find something more up in the trenches."

Half an hour later the tank went lumbering back toward the oasis. Fastening a halter-rope about his prisoner's neck, Price loosed his ankles and conducted him to a hiding-place among the tumbled masses of lava half a mile down the *wadi*. Kreor limped and grumbled, but he could walk.

Fastening him again, Price returned and searched the abandoned battlefield for food and water, finding all he could carry.

For two days Price kept the Arab bound, nursing his wounds with painful care. On the late afternoon of the second day, when Price was sleeping, the man worked loose his bonds.

Disturbed by some obscure warning of danger, perhaps some faint sound of the snake-man's footsteps or his breathing, Price looked up to see Kreor standing above him, a jagged mass of lava raised in both hands.

163

18. FROST OF GOLD

SNATCHING at the ancient battle-ax, which he kept always beside him, Price rolled over, away from the boulder in whose shadow he had been lying. The stone came crashing down where his head had been.

With a single gliding movement, Price was on his feet, swinging up the ax. The Arab made to leap forward, then, realizing his helplessness against the ax, stopped and folded his arms and stood staring at Price with mad hatred in his eyes.

Resolutely, Price met his stare.

"Slay me, Iru," the Arab muttered. "Strike, that I may be gathered into the abyss of the snake."

"Nothing doing. But tonight you are going to take me to Aysa. If you are able to murder me you are able to walk. We have plenty of moonlight. If you try any tricks it will be time enough to split your head."

The man assented with an apparent meekness that Price found disturbing.

"Very well, Iru. Since the gods awakened you, I shall not attempt to betray you again."

Price knotted the halter-rope about the man's neck, to preclude any attempt at flight. They finished the remaining water and food, and then set off across the lava-fields, toward the mountain looming dark in the moonlight.

It was five miles directly to the mountain; perhaps eight or nine by the route they took around to the north cliffs. Price held the rope, forced his guide to walk in front. The man limped somewhat, and it was past midnight when they reached the precipice.

The moon was low; it was dark in the shadow of the mountain. It would be impossible, Kreor said, to make the climb in darkness. They lay down to rest on bare lava. The Arab breathed loudly, and seemed to sleep, while Price kept his grasp on the ax, and fought slumber.

He held the rope tight. Toward dawn it loosened; he knew Kreor was creeping upon him, and jerked the rope. The Arab sprawled on the rock beside him, protesting that he had risen merely to stretch his muscles.

With the first light of day they started inching a perilous way up a narrow chimney between basalt columns. The snake-man went first, Price following, the rope tied around his waist so that he could use both hands.

Half an hour of difficult climbing found them three hundred feet up the face of an almost vertical cliff. Kreor, above, gained a narrow edge where he could stand with hands free, and began a furious attempt to untie the knot at his throat.

Cunningly, he had chosen a moment when Price required all his fingers and toes to cling to the rock. It was a desperate race, with life for the stake; the rope untied, Kreor could readily push Price to a fall of several hundred feet.

Price drew himself up with reckless haste. The Arab loosened the first knot; but Price, in anticipation of something of the kind, had tied several.

At last, trembling and panting from his effort, Price reached a crevice where he could free a hand. He seized the rope, jerked on it, almost precipitating the snake-man from the ledge.

"Lead on," Price commanded. "And keep the rope tight."

Snarling with baffled hate, the Arab wriggled crabwise into a narrow crack above the ledge. Following him, but keeping the rope taut, Price reached the ledge, and slipped through the crevice into a tiny, gloomy cavern.

Kreor led the way from one damp, black chamber into another. Light of day was swiftly lost; the darkness became abysmal. Walls and roof and floor were rugged, uneven stone. Sometimes the passages were difficult to push through. Twice they had to crawl for a distance upon hands and knees.

Again and again Price warned his guide to keep the rope tight. He kept asking the man whispering questions, so that the answers would reveal his whereabouts.

They came at last into a larger cavern. Price could not estimate its size in the utter darkness, but the faint sounds of their movements came whispering back to straining ears as if from the walls of a vast chamber.

Price counted two hundred and sixty paces, as the Arab, at the end of the stretched rope, led him through mystic darkness. He was attempting to remember distances and direction of turns, so that if he indeed found Aysa, he could bring her safely out.

"Here we enter the passage, Iru," Kreor said.

"Will there be men near?"

"I think not. These passages are remote."

"Come back this way."

Price tugged at the rope, led the man back into the cavern. Kreor uttered a howling scream.

"Silence!" Price hissed. "I'm not going to kill you. Lie down!"

He struck a match to see that the man had obeyed. Then he gagged him, with a handkerchief in his mouth and a *kafiyeh* tied around his head.

"Get up," he ordered. "And lead on to Aysa. I'll turn you loose if I get out with her."

With sullen reluctance, Kreor led the way from the rugged cavern to a smooth-floored, narrow tunnel. Cool damp air flowed outward through it; it was, Price supposed, intended for ventilation.

A hundred and eighty paces, and the snake-man turned to the left. They entered a wider passage, still completely dark. With a sure step the Arab led the way down it.

Green light glowed suddenly on a black wall before them, shadows danced in it, magnified, fantastic.

With a jerk of the rope, Price stopped his guide.

"What's that?" he demanded. Then, realizing that Kreor could not reply: "Let's get out of sight. Quick!"

The man stood still. Price was helpless. He had no idea which way to seek safety. And any struggle to make the Arab do his bidding would alarm whoever was approaching.

Three men in hooded robes of blue entered the dark hall, fifty yards ahead, from an intersecting passage. Two carried long, yellow-bladed pikes; the third, a torch flaring with a queer, vivid green flame.

Kreor made a futile attempt to scream through his gag. Price jerked savagely on the rope, and fondled the helve of his ax.

The three paused in the tunnel, the torch-bearer speaking.

The two pike-men laughed a little, as if at some idle jest. And then the three started on in the opposite direction.

The green light, flickering on walls and floor and roof, framed them. Dark figures in a little square of green. The square grew small. Then the light was gone; the passage had turned.

"Lead on," Price whispered. "And don't try again to give the alarm."

Again they were advancing in the darkness. The Arab seemed to require no light. Price kept the rope tight, counted paces. Kreor turned again to the left, into a passage that sloped sharply downward and curved smoothly to the left.

The slope, Price estimated, was one foot in four. By counting his paces, he could roughly calculate the amount of actual descent.

When he first became aware of the yellow light, they had descended eight hundred yards along the inclined passage. That meant that the spiral tunnel had carried them some six hundred feet downward, and perhaps three hundred feet below the level of the surrounding plain.

A vague, golden radiance arose; at first almost imperceptible. As they descended through the silent passage, the Arab leading sullenly at the end of his rope, it became denser, became a yellow fog of tiny, xanthic atoms, dancing endlessly.

He could see the walls of the passage, now, black basalt of the old volcano's core, smoothly chiseled, the tool marks almost undistinguishable. The tunnel was perhaps eight feet wide, somewhat higher, curving downward in a great spiral.

They were, by Price's estimate, two hundred feet lower in the yellow-lit passage, when they passed the end of a horizontal tunnel. When they were only a few yards beyond, Price heard voices from below. A man's and a woman's. Sharp, excited, angry.

"Come back," he snarled to Kreor.

He made the Arab enter the horizontal way. It was the same size as the other. Lucent, glistening yellow mist filled it with shadowless radiance.

Golden mist. The phrase throbbed suddenly in Price's brain. The snake-man had told him that Aysa slept, deep in the mountain, in golden vapor that was changing her to living metal. Was this weird light his golden mist? Was his fantastic story true?

As Price followed the sullen Arab along the tunnel, he noticed an extraordinary thing about its walls. They were covered with yellow frost. Over the smoothly hewn, jet-black basalt was a rime of glittering crystals, a delicate tracery of golden flakes. Even the floor was dusted with it. Golden frost!

It was amazing. The gleaming crystals, he knew, must have been deposited from the yellow mist. That meant that the mist was some volatile compound of actual, metallic gold, formed, probably, in the natural laboratory of the volcanic fissures beneath the mountain.

Price roughly understood the process of petrification, in which every minutest cell and tissue of an animal may be perfectly replaced with mineral, to endure as geologic records for a million years. It was easy enough to see how such a process might turn an animal—or a human being—into gold.

169

But could it take place without destroying life?

Obviously not, if the tissues were replaced with pure gold. But this yellow vapor was not pure gold. To exist in the form of vapor at such temperatures, it must be roughly as volatile as water.

Water is the basis of life, of all protoplasmic compounds. Was this yellow mist a compound of gold, distilled in the vast natural retort of the volcano, that could replace the water in the body, without upsetting any chemical balance? The idea was astonishing, but not impossible.

Busy with this conjecture, Price had almost forgotten the gagged man at the end of his rope. And suddenly he discovered that the rope was slack in his hands. He had come out of the tunnel, upon a narrow, stone-railed balcony. Beyond and below was sheer space, gold-misted.

From beside the tunnel's entrance, the snake-man leapt upon him with silent ferocity.

19. FOR THE MASTERY OF THE SERPENT

IT WAS sheer instinct for Price to drop the end of the rope tied to the Arab's neck, as he leapt back before that unexpected attack, and swung up the great ax to defend himself. And Kreor must have been expecting something of the kind, for he turned suddenly from the suicidal charge and bolted up the gold-frosted passage, coiling the rope as he ran.

Price sprang into instant pursuit, but the snake-man's limp seemed miraculously cured. He dashed back along the passage, gaining steadily, and disappeared where it gave into the spiral way.

Reaching the sloping tunnel only a few moments later, Price peered up and down through dancing golden mists. The Arab had vanished, soundlessly.

Cursing his carelessness in allowing Kreor to escape, Price could not help a certain admiration for his late prisoner. To be sure, the Arab was the acolyte of the insidious Malikar, the branded adherent of an evil snake-cult; he had tried to murder Price at every opportunity. It was his very determination and ruthless enterprise that had won him Price's regard as a worthy opponent.

While Price knew the man would hasten to spread an alarm, he could not be wholly sorry to see him escape.

For a moment Price stood at the end of the passage, uncertain whether to return to the balcony where Kreor had escaped, or to go on down the slanting way. Curiosity drew him back to the balcony; it was a strange and wonderful sight he had glimpsed from it in the brief second before the Arab's flight and his own pursuit.

The balcony was twenty feet wide and twice as long, with a low stone railing. Beyond the railing was a Cyclopean space, a circular room, fully four hundred feet in diameter, hewn in the living rock. The roof was a vast unbroken dome, yellow-crusted, like the walls, with frost of gold.

That colossal, rock-hewn room was filled with sparkling yellow mist. The immensity and strangeness of it awed Price. Almost timidly he crept to the edge of the high gallery and looked over the railing.

The floor was hundreds of feet below. Frosted, like the walls, with a glitter of yellow crystals, it filled a great half-circle, opposite him. The side of the amazing room directly below the gallery had no floor. The gold-rimmed rock ended in a ragged line. Below was cavernous space, a far-flung void filled with mist. Mile upon awesome mile—or so it seemed—it fell beneath him, golden-green with depth upon illimitable depth.

The circular room was hewn in the basalt, above the great cave. And half the room had only that cave for a floor. A colossal temple it was, above the natural laboratory in whose volcanic crucibles was born the puzzling golden vapor.

Leaning over the gold-frosted stone parapet, Price saw the bridge, a narrow span of black stone, flung across that sheer, golden-green abyss. From the wall, directly under his gallery, it leapt across to meet the ragged edge of the floor, near the center of the vast room. Incredibly narrow, it was little more than a black line from his point of view.

The room was like a theater. The half a floor was the

172

stage. The abyss that the narrow bridge spanned was the orchestra pit—with the bottom fallen out. The high balcony upon which Price stood was a lone box.

Price was still looking over the railing when the actors came upon that stage, to perform a weird and amazing drama.

Side by side they strode from the square opening of a rock-hewn passage, out upon the yellow-crusted floor. Malikar and Vekyra. So far below they looked like puppets.

Malikar, the golden man whom Price had twice fought. Thick-bodied, yellow-bearded, robed in crimson and wearing a red skull-cap. Coiled in one great hand was a thick, long whip.

Price had not seen Vekyra before, save in those extraordinary projections upon the sky. Her exotic beauty, wild and passionate, was almost startling. Slim, yellow-limbed, her body was cased in green. Red-golden hair was bound with a wide black band. Lids of oblique, tawny-green eyes were darkened; lips and cheeks and fingers reddened.

The two walked a little apart, and they seemed to be quarreling; Price knew at once that it was their voices he had heard upon the spiral way. Their voices reached him, Vekyra's high and clear, even in anger; Malikar's harshly unpleasant.

The words of their conversation, however, Price did not understand. They spoke rapidly; the sound was swallowed in the ringing echoes of the vast room. He was not sure even that they spoke a familiar language.

The woman ran suddenly away from Malikar, and up

173

the ramp that led to a stone platform, suggestive of an altar, set within a niche at the end of the great stage.

Price had not noticed the platform in detail before. Now, for the first time, he saw the snake. The real golden reptile whose dread reflection he had seen in the mirage. Huge, motionless, golden scales gleaming in the unshadowed light. Coiled in a heap of gleaming, undulating loops, the graceful pillar of its bright neck lifted in the center.

Vekyra stopped on the edge of the altar before it, and began to sing. She flung up bare yellow arms in the golden light. Her voice was keen, liquidly and tantalizingly sweet. And the song had a queer, archaic rhythm.

The evil, triangular head of the serpent swayed in time to Vekyra's singing, and the purple-black eyes watched her, smoldering with immemorial flames. Slowly the head was thrust out toward Vekyra, sank to the level of her shoulders.

The song stopped, then, and she ran up to it. Her yellow arms slipped around the motionless, horizontal column of the neck, in strange caress. She stroked the flat golden head.

Then Price heard Malikar's angry shout. Evidently displeased with what was happening, he was stalking belligerently toward the platform, swinging the heavy whip.

Springing suddenly away from the serpent, Vekyra ran down the ramp to meet him, calling out to the snake behind her with a strange, pealing shout.

The snake uncoiled its bright, undulating length; it glided after her down the ramp. It was, Price saw, fully the size of the largest boa; its length, he estimated, was at least fifty feet.

Vekyra stopped at the foot of the ramp, and the snake swept past her, toward Malikar. The triangular head was high, mouth yawning, bright tongue flickering, twin golden fangs gleaming evilly. And the snake hissed as it struck at Malikar; a sibilant, menacing roar, astonishingly loud, reverberating eerily in the vast temple.

Malikar stood boldly in its path, shouted with a voice like a brazen clang.

The serpent stopped, arrested before him. Still it hissed, angrily, tempestuously. Vekyra ran after it, calling out in a high, urgent tone. The snake struck, drove its fanged head at Malikar.

With surprizing alertness, the priest leapt back, and swung the black whip. It cracked like a pistol. The flat head recoiled, as if hurt. Malikar strode forward, brandishing the whip. He began to shout at the serpent, his voice brazen, ringing.

The snake writhed back before him, its hiss sinking to an uncertain whisper of hate.

Vekyra ran in beside it. Her slim yellow arms caressed its scales again. Her voice rose in silver, liquid peals.

The serpent stopped its retreat. The broad head whipped back and rubbed against the woman's golden body, caressingly. She stroked it.

Malikar came on. Vekyra spoke to the snake, appealingly, cajolingly, commandingly. The golden wedge of the head left her body and struck again at Malikar, but hesitantly, doubtfully.

Still the priest was shouting. The snake seemed to shrink from his harsh, brazen tones; the hate-filled hissing died. It

175

started to writhe away. Malikar bellowed savagely; it stopped.

He strode up to its shrinking coils, stood roaring at it. He struck it with the whip. A tremor ran along its glistening length; the weird, purple-black eyes remained fixed upon him. Again he lashed it, and it did not stir.

Vekyra ran up to it, began caressing its coils again, her voice eloquent with golden pleading. It paid her no heed; the black eyes remained upon Malikar.

At length the priest dropped his whip, boomed a harsh command. Slowly, hesitantly, the flat, yellow-scaled head was thrust out at him, its fanged mouth closed. With heavy open hand he slapped it a dozen times, so hard that Price, in his high gallery, heard the blows.

Then Malikar shouted a harsh order at it. The great head moved toward the woman. She cried out, silvery tones shaken, plainly terrified. The slow movement did not cease. The snake hissed again, with the whisper of a far wind.

Vekyra screamed brokenly, as if with extreme terror. She fled across the yellow-frosted floor, toward the passage through which she and Malikar had come. After her the great serpent glided swiftly, hissing.

She vanished. The snake stopped. Malikar called to it, and it came undulating back to him, silent. Before him it drew into a mound of shimmering golden coils and lowered its flat head, watching the priest with purple-black eyes.

Malikar began to lash it.

The whip was long, thick as his wrist at the butt, tapering. He swung it expertly. The thin tip touched the snake with explosive reports. It quivered; uneasy undulations ran along its bright coils, but the purple-black eyes did not cease their unwinking gaze. Sometimes the yellow man chuckled, thickly, evilly, as if he got a sadistic pleasure from the torture.

At last he stopped, and stood motionless a long time, staring at the snake. Then he pointed with the butt of the whip at the altar-like platform, shouted brazenly. The yellow, gleaming serpent glided back up the ramp, coiled itself in the niche again, unmoving.

Malikar coiled the whip. Swinging it in one hand, he crossed the floor to the brink of the golden-green abyss, and started over the narrow bridge. Fully two hundred feet long, unrailed, the bridge was no more than two feet wide. Beneath was the giddy void, luminous, vast as the gulf between suns.

With steady stride, the red-robed priest walked the dizzy bridge, until he was midway across the awful pit. Suddenly he halted. Price thought at first that he must have been overcome with vertigo. But he casually transferred the coiled black whip to his left hand, and absently, unconcernedly, scratched his head.

Then Malikar turned hastily, as if he had forgotten something. He walked back to the ragged edge of the floor, and across it, and vanished along the way Vekyra had taken.

177

20. THE SLEEPER IN THE MIST

THE strange duel of Vekyra and Malikar, for control of the golden serpent, had held Price engrossed. For the moment he had completely forgotten his escaped prisoner. For the moment he had completely forgotten his escaped prisoner, Kreor, who was certain to return as soon as he could find aid. As Malikar went out of view Price awoke to the fact that he must quit the gallery quickly if he wished to continue his free adventures in the mountain.

A glance told him there was only one way to leave the gallery: the passage through which he had come. He hastened back along it, resolving, as he went, to carry on his exploration of the yellow-lit corridors.

Kreor had told him that Aysa lay somewhere down here, sleeping. Price had no belief in the snake-man's veracity. The story had an element of weird incredibility; but at least, he supposed, the girl was as likely to be here as anywhere else.

He had reached the spiral passage, started cautiously downward, when he heard footsteps ahead of him, and angry, low-voiced muttering. Retreating hastily to the end of the horizontal passage, he entered it and flattened himself against the wall.

Malikar strode past in a moment, a scowl on his yellow face, grumbling under his breath. Wondering how soon he would return, Price waited until all sound from him had ceased, then entered the sloping way again, and ran down it, ears straining for sound of the alarm that Kreor must be spreading.

The quivering golden atoms in the air became thicker as he descended, until he moved through pallid wraiths of shining mist. Even then he noticed an odd tickling sensation in his nostrils, a slight breathlessness. But in his preoccupation with other perils he disregarded the menace of the yellow mist.

The tunnel became straight, level. Price followed it into the great, circular room he had surveyed from the high gallery. Curving, gold-frosted walls rose about him, to the dome hundreds of feet above. High under the dome he made out the balcony, through golden haze.

The ragged edge of the yellow-dusted floor was two hundred feet away. Beyond that edge was sheer space, with the single narrow span of the bridge leaping across to the wall beneath the high gallery. At the end of the bridge, he saw a great niche in the wall, a wide shelf above the abyss.

On his right, eighty yards across the floor, was the altar-like dais, with the glittering gold serpent upon it. At first realization that he had come into the lair of the snake, Price started back apprehensively into the passage.

But the yellow reptile's flat head was resting quietly upon the bright coils. The dread, purple-black eyes were closed. It seemed unaware of his entrance.

The slender bridge drew Price with a sort of fascination. He feared to set foot upon it; knew that he could not easily keep his head above that stupendous chasm of green-gold vapor. But he had a sudden conviction that Aysa must be in the niche beyond it.

It was not a time to hesitate. Malikar, for all he knew,

might return at any moment. Kreor would doubtless soon be back with a party to search for him. Worse, the gigantic snake might discover his presence.

Without pausing for any deliberate consideration of his position, Price slipped as silently as he could across the great floor, to its uneven edge at the center of the room. The snake remained motionless. He reached the bridge, set out across it.

Smooth, unrailed, the walk was less than two feet wide. Below was the sheer and awful void, shining immensities of golden-green.

A professional acrobat, with trained sense of balance, would have found the crossing no feat at all. But Price reeled. He felt a moment of nausea, had to shut his eyes to recover his balance.

He tried not to look into the pit, tried to keep his eyes on the yellow-rimmed stone at his feet. But the abyss drew his gaze with a sinister fascination.

He hurried, sometimes half running. His stomach was queerly light. Cold sweat pearled his face. He was panting, gripping his fists until nails cut into palms.

Dizziness seized him again, a sickening wave of it. He stopped to recover himself. Fiercely he willed to forget the yawning, misty void. He tried to think of Aysa. Of the night the Arabs had captured her and bartered her to Joao de Castro. Of their midnight escape from the caravan. Of their sweet, brief days in the hidden garden of Anz.

Head clear again, he hastened on.

Price was midway across the gulf when he was first

definitely aware of sleep descending upon him. When he first came into the thicker golden vapor he had noticed a curious tickling in his nostrils, a shortness of breath.

Now it was overcoming him like a rising sea. His limbs were suddenly weary, leaden-heavy. Weights pressed down his eyelids. His brain was slow and confused.

Alarmed, he stumbled on through the fog.

With a sigh of vague relief, he staggered across a gold-frosted floor, safely beyond the chasm. He had gained the niche. But the sleep of the thick yellow mist was beating upon him in waves. Beating him down . . . down . . . down. . . .

With chill certainty of dread, he knew that he could not keep awake to cross that fearsome bridge again, where a single false step would send him hurtling into limitless space.

He tried to pull himself together, surveyed the great niche. Its floor was semi-circular, with a radius of perhaps forty feet; and black, yellow-frosted rock arched above the recess.

Within it stood four great oblong slabs of gold-rimed stone, like massive tables. Three of them were empty. But on the fourth lay a sleeping figure, wrapped in garments that glittered with fine crystals of gold.

An eager, poignant pain in his heart, Price ran to the slab, and looked fearfully down at the quietly breathing figure.

The sleeper was Aysa.

The girl's lovely face, like her garments, was covered

with fine crystals of yellow frost. His heart checked with sudden despair, Price tenderly brushed one cheek. To his vast relief, the dust of gold came away, leaving soft white skin.

Perhaps she was being slowly transformed to living metal. But if so, the uncanny change was not yet apparent.

"Aysa! Aysa! Wake up!" he called, and shook her; but she did not stir.

The aureate vapor was obviously somniferous. The girl was sunk in the same unnatural slumber that he felt descending upon himself.

He lifted her body. It was completely relaxed, surrendered to oblivion. She was warm, breathing regularly. But he could not wake her.

Black despair fell upon him, made only keener by the possession of the lovely girl in his arms. He had found her—only to find with her inevitable defeat. But for the increasing influence of the soporific vapor, he could have carried her out and up to clear air, where she might wake normally. But he dared not set out across the narrow bridge, with the frightful risk that his abnormal slumber would hurl them both to death.

Price was still standing beside the slab of stone, Aysa's shoulders lifted in his arms, fighting the sinister sleep of the golden mist, and staring across the bridge he did not dare attempt to cross, when he saw Malikar.

The black whip still coiled in his hand, the red-robed priest was striding across the floor beyond the abyss, toward the end of the bridge.

Price's first impulse was to drop the girl, try to hide. Then he was sure that the golden man must already have seen him. And, if not, he would immediately observe that Aysa had been moved, the yellow dust brushed from her face.

Carefully he laid the unconscious girl back upon the rock table. He waited at the end of it, standing, fingers on the helve of the ancient ax. Malikar reached the bridge and started across.

Grim despair rose in Price's breast, and mute, helpless rage at fate. Why must this insidious sleep steal upon him, just when he had won his way to the girl? Why must Malikar return just now, to crown disaster? The Durand luck—was it mocking him?

His body felt very heavy. His breathing was slow, difficult; the yellow mist still tickled his nostrils. His eyes were leaden. And waves of sleep beat about him, long slow breakers from the ocean of oblivion.

He fought to keep his eyes open, focussed on the burly yellow priest striding so confidently across the bridge. He struggled for mastery over his body, even to deal one blow with Iru's ax. But the breakers of sleep rolled higher . . . flowed over him . . . drew him down into oblivion.

21. AT THE MERCY OF MALIKAR

FROM the sleep of the yellow fog, Price woke upon utter darkness. Stripped naked, he lay upon a little pile of straw or coarse grass, that was painful to his skin. Leaping up in uncomprehending alarm, he drove his head against a low stone ceiling.

Dazed, he sank back to his knees, and explored the narrow space about him with his hands. It was a narrow dungeon, some four feet wide and seven long, the roof so low that he could not stand. The walls were cold stone, roughly hewn. The door was a metal grating, through which breathed stagnant, vitiated air. His exploring fingers found nothing in the cell save the pile of moldy straw.

Sickness of despair settled upon him. He was the helpless captive of Malikar. The fact that his misfortune might have been foreseen from the beginning of his mad adventure in the mountain made it no easier to accept.

He tried to shake the metal grille. It seemed immovable; he could not even rattle it. He shouted through it, then. His voice echoed strangely through dark corridors, until it was swallowed in silence.

Baffled, helpless, he flung himself down again on the straw. He was hungry. His mouth was dry and bitter with thirst.

He was entombed within the mountain, apparently forgotten. A man marooned upon an alien planet would not be more completely isolated, he thought—and would at least have the advantage of interesting surroundings to divert his attention.

Time crept past, unnumbered weary hours, while he endured the torture of thirst and hunger, and plumbed the ultimate desolation of despair.

He slept again, and green light awakened him, streaming through the bars. Three blue-robed men were without, armed with pikes and *yataghans*, one carrying a green-flaring torch.

One of them unlocked the grille, pushed through two pottery bowls, of which one held water, the other a stew of meat thickened with flour. While the men waited, Price drained the one, avidly attacked the other.

When the bowls were empty, the snake-men unlocked the door again; one commanded harshly: "Come!"

They conducted him along the dark corridor, up a sloping, spiral way like that he had followed down to the serpent's lair, and finally through a wide, arched passage into an amazing room. A long chamber, hewn from the mountain's black volcanic mass. A score of feet wide, three times that long, with high, vaulted ceiling. The first thing about it that struck Price as strange was that it was illuminated by shaded electric lamps.

Along either wall stood a dozen snake-men, in blue, rigid, staring straight before them, armed with pikes and *yataghans*.

In the farther end of the room sat Malikar. Beneath a cluster of frosted electric globes, he sat behind a heavy mahogany desk, that might have come from some Manhattan office. Upon the desk was an electric fan, whirring noisily, and beside it lay the long black whip with which the priest had castigated the snake.

In crimson robe and skull-cap, the yellow man sat with thick golden hands resting on the desk. The strange eyes in his harsh face, shallow, tawny, watched Price from the moment of his entrance.

Along the stone wall behind Malikar were green-painted steel filing-cabinets, bookcases filled with volumes bound in the Occidental style, and a long bench scattered with scientific instruments—compound microscope, balances, test-tubes, re-agents, camera, brass telescope.

Above was a large wall-map of the world, dated 1921, with the imprint of a famous American publishing house.

Those scraps of Western civilization were as amazing to Price as any of the weird wonders he had encountered in the hidden land. And Malikar seemed to read his astonishment, as the snake-men stopped him before the desk.

"Surprized to find me a cosmopolitan, eh?" the yellow priest asked in his dead voice. And the language was English.

"Yes," Price said. "I'm surprized."

"You are English, aren't you?"

"American."

"Ah. I visited New York ten years ago. An interesting city."

Price stared at him.

"I've been going abroad rather frequently, since about the time of the fall of Rome," the yellow man added. "My last trip was in 1921-22. I spent a few months at Oxford and Heidelberg, to acquaint myself with the latest developments of your crude civilization, and returned home around

186

the world, by way of your country. I use a disguise, of course, that I don't find necessary here.

"By the way, I believe you followed my route in here from the sea?"

"You mean the road of skulls?"

"Precisely. The human skull is an enduring marker, with high visibility.—But now I'd like some information about yourself, and the circumstances to which I am indebted for your call."

Price flushed at the mocking irony in his cold tones.

"What's you name?"

"Price Durand."

"You are aware that you have been mistaken for an ancient ruler named Iru—whose tomb you appear to have rifled?"

"Perhaps so."

The shallow, eyes regarded Price fixedly.

"Mr. Durand, you might explain the purpose of your visit."

Price hesitated, decided to speak. There was no need of caution; nothing could make his circumstances any more hopeless.

"I was looking for Aysa. The girl you abducted."

"I am glad you are honest, at least," the golden man mocked him. "But, unfortunately for you, the young woman has been selected to fill a higher destiny than you planned for her. She is to be priestess of the snake—and my consort."

"Are you turning her to gold?" Price demanded flatly, controlling his anger.

"The snake would accept no ordinary human as its priestess," Malikar informed him, tauntingly. "She must be of the golden blood.

"Don't you understand the transformation? The yellow mist in the lair of the snake is a rare auriferous compound, formed in the volcanic heart of the earth. Condensing upon the walls of the temple, it forms yellow frost.

"When inhaled into a living body, this compound replaces the water in the protoplasm, forming a living substance, the color of gold, that is far stronger and more enduring than common flesh."

"And you expect Aysa to give herself to you?" Price angrily demanded. "You know she hates you—deservedly!"

"I fear her regard for me is not of the kindest," Malikar leered. "But once of the golden blood, she will not easily escape me. She can not seek death. Taming her may be pleasant sport—and time is nothing to the lucky immortals. She will learn to love me."

Malikar leaned forward, chuckling throatily. He picked up the heavy black whip on the desk, ran the thin lash of it through his yellow fingers, gloatingly, sugestively.

Red rage flared up in Price at thought of lovely Aysa, locked in a golden body from which she could not escape, the slave and plaything of this leering yellow demon.

He glared at Malikar, speechless with anger, longing savagely to sink his fingers into the yellow priest's thick neck.

Suddenly the golden man bent, opened a drawer of the desk, and produced a delicate brush and a small bottle of what appeared to be liquid, flowing gold. Setting brush and vial on the desk, he looked up at Price with flat, inscrutable, yellowish eyes.

"Mr. Durand," he said suavely, "I am going to offer you an unusual opportunity. I can make use of your services in exterminating the foolish gold-seekers that came with you in here."

"Will you free Aysa——" Price began eagerly.

"No," Malikar grated shortly. "But I give you one chance to save your pitiful life."

"And that is——"

"Here is your choice: Swear allegiance to the snake, and to me, priest of the snake. I will paint the symbol of the snake upon your forehead, spare your life to the service of the snake."

"I'll do nothing of the kind——"

"This is your choice," repeated Malikar, with grim irony. "Become slave of the snake, and live. or you shall be the slave of *this* snake"—he lifted the black coils of the whip—"and die in the dungeon!"

The jeering cruelty of the hard, flat voice snapped Price's control of himself. Red anger swept him. Naked as he was, he turned upon the snake-man beside him, snatched the golden-bladed pike from his dumfounded grasp, and leapt savagely toward the red-robed man behind the desk.

Two guards seized him before he had moved three steps.

Malikar sprang from behind the big desk, chuckling unpleasantly and drawing the whip's thin lash through his fingers.

"Loose the dog," he snapped at the guards, in Arabic.

They released Price, leapt back to the walls.

Again he darted forward, the pike uplifted.

The thin black length of the whip reached out, writhing like a living tentacle. It did not touch Price; it wrapped around the wooden haft of the pike.

The weapon was snatched from Price's hand, flung across the floor. Still he ran forward, fists clenching, driven by blind, mad rage at this suave, taunting golden demon.

Again the whip leapt out, with a sharp report. In his red anger Price was unconscious of the pain. But the skin on his chest was slashed open as if with a knife.

Still he ran on, fists doubled to drive into Malikar's body.

As if endowed with malignant life, the whip reached out again, coiled around his ankles. Tripped by it, he stumbled, fell heavily.

As he staggered to his feet, the lash drew a cold line of pain across his naked back. Again he stumbled forward.

The long lash went round and round his body, pinioning his arms. Malikar jerked it, sent him spinning once more to the floor.

As Price dragged himself to his feet, he saw that the golden tiger had entered the long hall behind him. In its black *howdah* sat Vekyra the yellow woman, watching him with slanted, tawny-green eyes—detached, impersonal, pitiless.

Again the lash fell across his shoulders, like a slashing blade. Price heard Malikar chuckle thickly, in evil, sadistic pleasure. He turned and ran reeling back at the priest, grasping with vain hands at the living, torturing whip.

22. VEKYRA'S GUEST

PRICE'S savage rage against the torturer was drowned in the blood that ran thickly down his naked body from the slashes of the whip. He realized suddenly that he was merely giving Malikar the pleasure of killing him, uselessly.

He checked his last charge at the golden man, stood motionless in the long hall, beneath the shaded electric lights that were so weirdly incongruous among the baffling wonders of this forgotten land.

Again the whip touched him, drew blood like a flashing blade; involuntarily he flinched. But he folded his arms and stood staring at Malikar.

"Enough, Mr. Durand?" the golden man mocked him.

Price bit his lip, said nothing.

Malikar gestured to the snake-men who had brought him into the room. They closed upon him—to take him back to the dank horror of the dungeon, he knew. And he knew he was not likely to leave it again, living.

Price turned, and saw the tiger again. Colossal golden cat, elephantine in bulk, it stood in the middle of the hall. The yellow woman, Vekyra, was leaning over the side of its black *howdah*, watching Price with odd speculation in her greenish eyes.

Desperate, illogical hope came to him abruptly. He knew that the woman and Malikar were at loggerheads. He had seen their duel for the control of the golden serpent. Vekyra, he suspected, was not delighted by Malikar's passion for Aysa.

191

Running suddenly ahead of his guards, toward the tiger, he cried:

"Vekyra, won't you help me?"

It was a hopeless prayer. She had watched while Malikar plied the whip. And he had seen no pity on her oval face.

Sick from the pain of his bleeding wounds, dizzy, reeling, Price was clutching at the last, futile straw of hope.

"Oh, Vekyra, you will help me! One so beautiful——"

At the last she smiled, brightly, enigmatically. Her greenish eyes showed interest, but no pity for him.

Price's guards hesitated behind him, keeping a respectful distance from the yellow tiger. Malikar roared after them: "Take the dog on to his dungeon!"

That harsh command had the effect upon Vekyra that Price had tried for in vain. The oblique eyes flashed maliciously green. She smiled down again.

"Stranger, you are my guest," her silvery voice spoke. "Mount with me."

She darted a venomous glance at Malikar.

"The man is mine," snarled the golden priest. "If I command that he rots in the dungeon, there he rots."

"Not," Vekyra insisted with a poisoned smile, "if I take him to my palace."

"Forward!" bellowed Malikar. "Seize the man."

Timidly the blue-robes advanced.

"Touch him," Vekyra assured them sweetly, "and the tiger dines well this night."

They paused, looking fearfully back at Malikar.

The golden priest strode down across the hall, the long

whip, red with Price's blood, writhing and hissing before him like a living serpent. The snake-men scattered toward the walls.

Vekyra laughed, and her laughter was chiming, silvery, mocking.

"Perhaps your whip can master the snake, O Priest," she called, "but not Zor, I think. The tiger has been mine too long."

Malikar hesitated visibly; but he came on toward Price, the whip twisting and cracking angrily before him.

Hardly able to stand, Price staggered toward the tiger. His raw wounds throbbed intolerably. Nausea and weakness almost overwhelmed him, the result of long days of hardship as much as of his present pain and loss of blood. The floor of the long hall swam and rocked, the high electric lights floated in fiery circles.

Vekyra leaned forward in the *howdah*. She whispered to the tiger; one great ear slanted back to listen.

Then the colossal golden beast advanced upon Malikar, crouching, hind legs drawn forward. It growled menacingly. The sound was a sullen roar, filling the great hall with throbbing fury.

Malikar stopped; the hissing lash dropped to the floor.

"Woman!" his voice grated, hard with hate, "you will pay for this. You think I will not whip you because you are of the golden blood?"

"I know you will not whip me—because you can not!"

"Know now that you are no longer priestess of the snake— nor can ever be again. Another has been chosen."

"Of that I had learned already," the woman responded,

193

wrath in her silver tones. "But perhaps I have found another to be priest of the snake and master of the golden folk. Was not Iru once as great as Malikar?"

She gestured toward Price with a slim golden arm.

"That whelp is not Iru," snarled the priest. "He is but a lying pretender, who rifled the king's tomb."

"And was Malikar not once a lying pretender?" the silver voice inquired acidly. And it took a note of warning: "Guard well your new priestess, Malikar, lest she fall into the pit, or perchance feed the snake, instead of worshipping it."

Again Vekyra leaned forward, calling something into the tiger's ear. The gigantic yellow beast crouched until its tawny belly touched the floor. With lithe grace the woman leapt from the *howdah*.

Running to Price's side, she slipped off the loose green cloak above her close-fitting tunic, wrapped it about his bleeding shoulders.

"Come!" she whispered urgently in his ear. "Mount before yon slave-driver devises more evil!"

Reeling uncertainly, Price turned with her toward the crouching tiger. A slim, bare yellow arm slipped about his smarting shoulders. Vekyra, amazingly strong, lifted him into the great *howdah*, where he fell back gratefully among the cushions.

Malikar ran back to his desk, hammered a great bronze gong behind it, whose screaming reverberations filled the hall with insistent clamor of alarm. Vaguely, his head spinning with pain and exhaustion, Price was aware of shouting and the clangor of arms along distant passages.

Vekyra, leaping easily into the *howdah* beside him, called again into the tiger's ear. The great beast surged to its feet with one smooth effort, far unlike the awkward lurching of a rising camel.

Vekyra shouted again, and the animal wheeled and ran from the room, the *howdah* swaying upon its back like a boat grasped in a mighty current.

Behind, Malikar bellowed ominously, "Woman, you shall taste my whip for this. And the dog upon which you defile your hands shall——"

Then they were outside in a dark passage, illuminated only by occasional flaring cressets—the electric lights appeared to have been restricted to the one room. It was eight feet wide, nearly twice that high; but there was none too much room for the racing tiger.

"We must hasten," Vekyra whispered, her voice edged with alarm, "or Malikar will have the gates closed, and shut us out of my palace."

A great, yellow-fringed ear was cupped back to listen, as Vekyra called another command. The tiger surged forward more swiftly, until Price's sensations were those of sheer flying. Around a sharp corner it flung, plunged swaying up a sloping way.

Ahead, Price saw an incandescent rectangle of sky, almost blindingly blue to eyes sensitized by gloom.

Vekyra reached down among the cushions beside her, found a short, oddly shaped metal bow. Snatching an arrow from a full quiver fastened in the corner of the *howdah*, she nocked it, sat waiting alertly.

Dark hastening figures were suddenly visible in the bright, enlarging rectangle ahead. Then it was narrowing.

197

Shrill squealing of pulleys reached Price's ears. Great valves of yellow metal, he saw, were swiftly closing.

Vekyra drew her arrow to the head. Price heard the singing *twang* of the bow, and ahead, a sharp cry. The screech of pulleys ceased.

The tiger slipped through the space between the half-closed gates, so narrow that the *howdah's* fastenings scraped. And they burst into sunlight so bright that Price, for a time, could see nothing.

Weak and dizzy, he sank back among the cushions, drawing an arm across his eyes. Then he felt Vekyra's smooth arms slipped beneath his shoulders.

"Be ye welcome," she whispered, "to my castle of Verl. Rest, and fear nothing, for you are Vekyra's guest."

She lifted him up, and her whisper became soft, seductively caressing, as she added, extravagantly: "I am your slave."

23. THE GOLDEN FOLK

FOR a few minutes, Price lay completely relaxed, supported by Vekyra's arm, as the tiger swayed forward. Hot, blinding sunlight drenched him, strangely grateful to one unexpectedly delivered from the dungeons of Malikar. Its penetrating force was mildly stimulating. Presently he moved to sit up, stirred by curiosity about this amazing, mountain-crowning palace.

Gorgeous wonders of Oriental gardens burst upon him. The tiger was pacing across a wide court, surrounded with walls and colonnades of refulgent gold and gleaming white marble. Dark, lush grass edged crystal pools, where white doves splashed joyously. Graceful palms flung high their emerald, tufted masses. Bright-flowering shrubs tinctured the air with cool fragrance.

About the broad court rose the gold-and-alabaster towers of Verl. Lacy balconies above vivid gardens, supported by slender, twisted columns. High, trefoil-arched windows, peering domes and slim minarets. The architecture was typically Arabic; but all was snowy marble, shining gold.

In the white dazzle of the afternoon sun the splendors of the place would have been painful, but for the cool green shadows of the gardens.

Deliberately the golden tiger carried the swaying *howdah* along a gravel path, beneath an arcade of palms. Price stared about him in silent wonder. The scene was so like his dreams of many cruel days that he felt suddenly that it must be illusion, madness, mirage.

Had his old delirium returned?

199

Summoning a desperate strength, he turned fiercely to the woman beside him in the *howdah*, seized a bare, golden arm, peered into her face. Her skin gleamed like pale gold; it felt somehow metallic. But it was warm and yielding beneath his fingers; he felt under it firm, vibrant muscles.

"Woman of gold," he demanded, "are you real?"

The face was strange. Oval. Exotically lovely. The color of pale gold, framed in hair of ruddy gold. The slightly slanted eyes were greenish, like the tiger's. Behind heavy golden lashes, they were enigmatic, inscrutable.

"More real than you are, Iru. For I am gold, and you are frail flesh. For I was as I am now, when Anz was living, and her people teeming millions. And I shall be as I now am when your bones are as the bones of Anz."

She smiled, and he read a baffling challenge in her eyes.

"Maybe so, old girl," Price muttered in English. "But I call your bluff, and I'll play the game."

His fighting will could keep back oblivion no longer. A sea of night flowed over him, and he sank back in Vekyra's arms.

Price awoke within the most magnificent—if perhaps not the most comfortable—room that he had ever occupied, huge and lofty, the broad doorway arched and silken-curtained. The marble floor was thick-strewn with rugs, deep-piled, dull-red and blue. High walls were milky alabaster, paneled with gold.

From his elaborate, canopied bed he could look through wide, unglazed windows, over the basalt walls of Verl, to the dark lava plateau half a mile below, which stretched away beyond the green mark that was the oasis of El Yerim, to tawny wastes of flat red desert beyond, to shimmering horizons smoky in hot distance.

Price was surprized by his sense of well-being, and by the fact that his whip-cuts were completely healed. Such recovery could not have taken place in one day. He guessed, and Vekyra later admitted, that he had lain for some days in oblivion induced by her healing drugs. For she, it seems, was something of a chemist and physician.

Somewhat to Price's confusion, he found six personal attendants waiting in the vast room on the day he woke. They were young women, tall, rather attractive, with the dark hair, thin lips, and aquiline noses that bespoke Arabic blood. They wore short, dark-green tunics, and each carried at her waist a long, crooked-bladed, golden *jambiyah*. On the forehead of each was the yellow brand of the snake.

They brought him white silken robes (his own garments were still in Malikar's possession), offered him food, water and wine. He tried a little to talk to them; but though they seemed pathetically eager to serve him, they avoided his questions.

Still feeling languid, without energy, he made no effort to leave the great room until late afternoon, when Vekyra came to call upon him. Her slim, pale-golden figure was cased in dark forest-green, her red-gold hair fell in a flaming cascade. The slant of her dark-lidded eyes gave a hint of mystery to her oval face.

Price rose to greet her. She saluted him as Iru, inquired about his health, and seated herself upon a cushioned sofa. The girls—Price was not yet certain whether they were servants or jailers—retired discreetly.

"One thing I must tell you," Price began abruptly. "You

201

called me Iru. I'm not. My name is Price Durand. I was born on the other side of the world."

Deliberately, the greenish, oblique eyes studied his face, his lean, muscular limbs. Price, still feeling the lassitude of convalescence, sat down opposite the golden woman.

"You are Iru, king of Anz," Vekyra said calmly, at length. "For I knew the ancient Iru well—who better? You are he. It makes no difference that you have been born again, and in a far land."

"You knew him, then?" He felt a keen interest in the old ruler for whom he had been several times mistaken. And he was determined not to show any awe of Vekyra.

"You have forgotten me? Then I shall tell you the story of the ancient Iru, for it is only the beginning of the same story that we are living now—you and I, Malikar and Aysa."

At the girl's name, Price started visibly.

Vekyra smiled obliquely, murmured: "Ah, I see you remember *her*."

"I know a girl of that name."

He tried to make his tone impersonal, but the woman must have caught some hint of his feeling, for her oval face went suddenly hard with hate.

"Aysa, like you, is born again!" she hissed. "Again we are all four together, to finish the story that started when Anz was young."

The passion went from her golden face as quickly as it had come, and she settled her gleaming body among the cushions and flung back the rich, glinting masses of her hair.

"When I was a girl—and not yet my blood golden—Iru

was king of Anz. The people loved him, because he was handsome and strong, famous for his courage and his skill with his golden ax. And you are he!"

Price shook his head.

"You have his lean, tall figure, his blue eyes, his red hair—and those are rare indeed among our people. More, I know your face!

"Anz was great then. The creeping drift-sands were yet far off. The rains came every winter; the lakes and reservoirs were always full, the crops and pastures plenty.

"Then there were no golden beings save the snake. The snake has lived in the mountain since before the dawn of man. It sometimes came out, through a cave, to hunt. The people of Anz thought it a god—for the strange fascination of its eyes—and built a temple to it below the mountain.

"In the time of Iru, Malikar was priest of the snake. A bold man he was, and a seeker of wisdom. As priests do, he knew the truth about his god. He went back into the cave, and found the abyss of golden vapor, which rises from the fires of inner earth, turning all things that breathe it into deathless gold.

"The snake was but a common reptile that had made its lair within the mountain and breathed the mist. No more god than any snake. Malikar made tests, and found the secret of the golden blood.

"Now you—or Iru—were a warrior and a hunter. You knew not the secret of the snake, but you held that it was an evil thing. You decreed that the toil and the lives of the Beni Anz should be paid it in sacrifice no longer. You ordered the priests to leave their temple. For this Malikar hated you, and resolved to destroy you, to make his god supreme and rule as both priest and king.

"Yet another quarrel had you and the priest. I, Vekyra, was then a young woman, a princess of Anz, and not golden, as you see me now. You loved me. You said, *then*, that I was beautiful. We were betrothed to marry. Malikar desired me also.

"Iru led his soldiers to the temple. The priests fled before his golden ax. He destroyed the temple and sealed the snake's cavern.

"Malikar fled when he saw the battle was lost, left the other priests. By a secret way he went into the mountain, and far down into the golden mist. There he slept for many days, until the golden vapor had penetrated his body, changed its tissues to strong and deathless gold.

"Now the girl Aysa was a slave. I bought her from traders of the north, for a tiring-maid. One day Iru saw her, and wanted her. Now since we were to marry, I was not pleased. I told him he might have the girl—if he would exchange for her a tamed tiger.

"While Malikar lay sleeping in the golden mist, Iru rode into the mountains and fought a tigress and brought back its cub. He tamed it and brought it to me, so I was forced to give him the slave, Aysa. But better for him had he kept his beast!"

Green, slanted eyes flamed.

"Malikar lay in the mountain until he was a man of gold. Then he led out the snake, and went among the desert clans that dwelt beyond Anz, to preach his new religion. He said he had died, and been born again—delivered of the snake, with a body of gold.

"The desert folk believed him. For was his body not golden, and so strong he let them hew it with swords? Malikar led them against Anz, the snake with him, to freeze men with the chill of its eyes.

"But you were a great warrior. You gathered the cattle and the tillers of fields inside the walls. Then you went out, with your warriors and Korlu, your ax, and scattered the desert men back into the waste.

"But Malikar and the snake you could not slay, for they were gold. You could only return to Anz, and close the gates against them.

"Then Malikar resolved to use cunning. He sent the snake back into the mountain. Painting his golden body, to make it the color of a man's—as he yet does, when he goes out into the world—he slipped back into Anz, to murder you.

"But you were surrounded by your warriors, and the great ax was always with you. Malikar could not approach you secretly.

"Then he found a new plan. He went to Aysa, the slave. How he won her, I do not know. Perhaps with the promise of gold, which was plenty in the cave of the snake. Perhaps with fear of the snake-god. Or it may be that his kisses were enough.

"Aysa put his poison in your bowl, and you drank it with your wine. You died. But the slave gained little by her treason. Iru tasted the poison, and knew what she had done, and slew her with the ax before he fell.

"Then Malikar stood forth as the man of gold and the avenger of the snake. Leaderless, the Beni Anz bowed down before him. They sent an offering of many slaves to the snake, and Malikar ruled them, priest and king.

"With the many slaves, Malikar hewed a new temple in the heart of the mountain, down in the very mist of gold.

"When Iru was dead, Malikar took me by force into the mountain, and left me sleeping in the yellow vapor until I was gold. He would have made me his slave for ever. But the tame tiger cub, that Iru had caught for the slave-girl's sake, followed me into the mountain.

"There the sleep fell upon it, and it also woke an animal of gold. Malikar could not kill it, and it still loved and served me. Year by year it grew larger—perhaps because it was not grown when it slept—until even the snake fears it.

"That is the story of the golden folk."

Price sat in silent wonder. He did not believe in reincarnation; but neither did he disbelieve. He knew that hundreds of millions hold it as the basis of their religion.

Vekyra's story was interesting. It had a strange plausibility. It seemed to explain much at which he had wondered. He was willing to admit it as possibly true—all of it save that Aysa was the avatar of a murderess.

Vekyra glided up from her couch, and across the rugs to Price. She leaned on the arm of his chair, her perfumed tresses falling like a torrent of flame across his shoulders, her green-clad body touching him.

"That is the story, Iru. And a hundred generations I have lived in this palace of Verl that Malikar built for me, enduring a life without love that had no mercy of death—waiting for you, my Iru!

206

"Many times I have longed to leap into the golden abyss. But I knew that some time you would be born again, my Iru, and come back to me—even though new lands rose from the sea, and new deserts barred your way."

The golden woman slipped down beside Price, her warm body vibrant against his own. Her slim yellow arms went around him, soft and yet strong. She lifted her enigmatic, oval face, greenish eyes burning, reddened lips parted in avid invitation.

A moment he hesitated, almost shrinking from her. Then the burning promise of her swept him away. He inclined toward her, flung his arm around her slender body. Her hot lips came up to his, clinging, hungry—and their touch plunged him into white, delicious flame.

24. MIRRORS OF MIRAGE

HEN Vekyra was gone, Price felt disturbed and a little guilty thinking of Aysa. But the golden woman had certainly saved his life, he reflected.

He might have found other excuses for his surrender to the golden beauty. Her good offices appeared the only possible means of Aysa's rescue—and a very doubtful means, Vekyra hating the unfortunate girl as she evidently did. Vekyra's displeasure would mean a speedy and probably permanent return to the dungeons of Malikar. But, honest with himself, Price admitted that no such consideration had occurred to him during that moment in Vekyra's arms.

Next morning, when Price had breakfasted, he went for a stroll about the palace, escorted by four of his female retinue. As he strode ahead of them through magnificent gardens and among gold and marble colonnades, his eye was alert for some opportunity to escape.

He had resolved to leave Verl, if that could be done. Vekyra, certainly, would not willingly or knowingly aid him in Aysa's rescue. But escape seemed a hopeless thing, unarmed as he was, and ceaselessly watched by the snake-branded women.

"*Effendi* Duran'!"

The hail, in a familiar voice, startled him. Turning, he saw the sheikh Fouad el Akmet approaching along an avenue of palms. The old Bedouin was unarmed, and beside him, familiarly close, tripped one of Vekyra's girls, crooked *jambiyah* at her waist.

"Peace be upon you, O sheikh," Price greeted him, and walked to meet him. "You are also the guest of Vekyra?"

The old Arab drew Price apart from the warrior-girls, and whispered through his scraggy black beard:

"Aywa, Sidi!" He looked cautiously at the waiting girls. "Three days ago the *Howeja* Jacob Garth sent me to scout toward the mountain, with my men. The evil golden woman-*djinni*, who rides the golden tiger, came upon us suddenly. Three of my men the tiger killed. And she brought me to this castle of Eblis."

The old sheikh glanced behind him again, lowered his voice further.

"But yet I may escape. The woman with me, *she* knows a *man*." He leered fatuously. "Nazira is her name. Last night she promised to aid me. I know my way with the women, eh?"

Price grinned. Fouad whispered again:

"Effendi, when the time comes, will you go with me? *Bismillah!* I like not to be alone in this land of *'ifrits!'*"

"Yes," Price assured him, though he was none too confident of the old Arab's ability to seduce his jailer, and still less confident that, even with the woman's aid, escape would be successful.

The Bedouin turned away, leering familiarly at the waiting girl. Price, with his escort, moved on, amid the splendors of Verl.

Presently Vekyra overtook him, upon the tiger. She made the golden beast crouch beside him, extended a slim yellow arm.

She had exchanged her green garments for a close-

fitting tunic of luminous violet, that shimmered metallically
when her lithe body moved. Her ruddy hair, fastened back
with a broad band of the same material, assumed a glowing brilliance against it.

"Iru," she said, "I wish you to ride with me this morn,
upon the mirage."

"Upon the mirage?"

"Yes. I am the mistress of the illusion. You have seen
it. A secret of ancient Anz. The old wise men mastered
the laws of illusion, contrived mirrors—and other forces—
to rule the mirage."

"How——"

"You shall see, in the hall of illusion."

She spoke to the tiger, and the gigantic cat, which
wore neither bridle nor halter, swung rapidly away, along
a magnificent colonnade of white marble and gold.

The woman arranged the cushions in the *howdah* and
drew Price down beside her. The swaying of the beast
threw him against her, so that he felt the strength of her
body, caught the heavy perfume of her hair.

The tiger carried them into the central pile of the castle,
and up a spiral ramp, that ascended, Price knew, into the
great middle tower of shimmering gold. Through unglazed
openings in the walls he glimpsed the white and gold
wings of the building, and below, the grim sea of dark
desert, blue in the haze of heat.

At last they entered a strange hall, at the very summit
of the tower. From the end of the sloping way the tiger
stepped silently and cautiously out upon a vast mirror, an
unbroken sheet of crystal that formed the floor.

Price gazed about in amazement at the hall of illusion. Not only its floor was crystal. The walls were mirrors, oddly shaped, strangely curved. Reflecting one another, they gave deceptive impressions of limitless vistas of mirrored halls, made it impossible to tell the actual size of the room. Half the roof was open to the turquoise sky, half a brilliant plane of flawless crystal.

A thousand times—ten thousand times—in mirror-walls and floor and ceiling, Price saw reflections of himself and Vekyra upon the tiger. Infinitely the image was repeated, sometimes looking gigantic, sometimes diminished almost to invisibility.

Vekyra reached out her hand and touched a little cluster of five tiny disks. Price had not seen them before; they seemed suspended in space beside the tiger. Actually, he realized, they projected through a sheet of crystal beside them, polished to the perfection of invisibility.

Vekyra pressed a crimson stud. Beneath, Price heard the even throb of concealed machinery. The mirrors shifted, spun; reflections swam disturbingly within them.

The thousand images of the tiger fled away astoundingly. A single level floor of blue, shimmering crystal reached out in all directions to infinity. Away across that bright plain raced the reflections of the tiger, shrank to tiny dark points, vanished.

Only the blue light of the sky was mirrored in the crystals; Price felt oddly as if the tiger were suspended in a blue and vacant void.

Vekyra touched a green disk. The shrill whine of another hidden mechanism rose about them. The air was suddenly charged, tense. Price sniffed the pungence of ozone, knew that powerful electric forces must be discharging about them.

"Watch!" cried Vekyra. "The bending of light, the birth of illusion!"

Price saw black points come into the mirrors, where their reflection had vanished; saw the points expand into dark lines of far horizons; scraps of distant desert, swimming swiftly nearer, so that he saw first blue haze above, then undulating ranks of yellow-red dunes; queer patches of desert; snatches of sand and sapphire sky. All mingled fantastically in a crazy-quilt of illusion, swiftly expanding, rushing nearer.

Abruptly, it all took form. The scraps of desert merged into a whole. Seemingly hundreds of feet below, a heavy slope of loose sand reared its barren yellow-red crest. Away to hot, shimmering world-rims rolled crescent dunes.

The illusion was incredibly real.

Price could see his own body, the golden woman beside him in the cushioned *howdah* . . . and far below, the sand-desert. The mountain, the dark surrounding lava flows, had vanished.

Vekyra smiled at him, as if in malicious delight at his amazement, and pressed a yellow disk. Then, though Price had no sensation of physical motion, the desert seemed to race beneath them. Vast, sun-glinting salt-pans flashed beneath, like snow-clad lakes. Yellow outcroppings of limestone. Barren plains of flint and clay. Black lava fields.

Price reached out an exploring hand toward the clustered disks. Where his eyes saw only empty air, his fingers met polished crystal. A queer, tingling shock made his arm jerk back involuntarily.

212

"Beware," warned Vekyra. "All the tower is charged with the power that bends down the light. And you are not immortal—*yet*."

She touched a green stud. And Price, looking over the *howdah's* edge again, saw that they seemed to hang motionless over the oasis of El Yerim.

A broad streak, green with date-palms, across dark lava plains. The clustered mud houses of the town. Across the lake, the camp of his recent allies.

White tents, grouped along the shore. The gray bulk of the tank—Sam Sorrows had got back safely. Supplies stacked, tarpaulin-covered. The black tents of Fouad's Bedouins, the herds of camels.

And two surprizing things. One was a set of glistening, parallel wires strung upon poles cut from palm trunks—an unmistakable radio antenna. The other was a smooth, cleared field on the gravel beyond the camp, with two airplanes squatting upon it. Trim, gray-winged military planes, machine-guns frowning grimly above their cockpits, light aerial bombs in their racks. Beside the fuselage of one of them he saw Jacob Garth, unmistable in his faded khaki and white *topi*, staring up at them.

For a moment Price was dumfounded. Then the explanation of it burst upon him. Garth had insisted, rather strangely, upon bringing no airplanes with them, his only excuse being the difficulty of landing in the sand-desert.

But he must have secretly arranged for the planes, left them in the hands of unsuspected allies. He had smuggled a portable radio transmitter in with the supplies, unknown to the rest of the party. The landing-field prepared, he had sent direction to the planes by wireless.

213

Now Price understood why Garth had been so ready to dynamite the schooner. With the planes, it was useless to him. Also, Price better understood Malikar's desire for his own aid against the treasure-seekers.

"Those are devices of war?" asked Vekyra, pointing to the planes.

"Yes. Men fly in them—to battle."

"You think they will again attack this mountain?"

"I'm sure they will. Jacob Garth isn't the sort to give up."

"Jacob Garth? He was your leader?"

"Not mine. But now he commands."

"Do you see him?"

"The large man, by that machine." Price pointed.

Vekyra studied him intently, nodded. "That is what I wished to know."

Her slim yellow arm reached from the *howdah*, touched the center disk.

The vibrant whine of hidden mechanisms, which Price had forgotten in his interest at what he saw, abruptly died. The scene below was shattered into a thousand fragments; into torn reflections in a thousand mirrors.

The shattered shards of images fled away. A moment the mirrors were blank, shimmering with the ultramarine brilliance of the sky. Then a thousand black dots were in them. Specks that swelled, rushed nearer, expanded into pictures of the tiger and its riders.

Softly the tiger padded across the floor of crystal, out of the hall of illusion.

25. THE CROWN OF ANZ

NEXT MORNING Price rose at dawn, to find three of his six female servants—or guards—waiting in his splendid room. They brought him breakfast; and, when he had eaten, and strolled out of the apartment, they followed him discreetly, keeping ten yards behind.

Again he roved the vast building in the hope of some discovery that would lead to a means of escape. Now that Jacob Garth had the airplanes, he would surely attack the mountain again, and with some chance of success. Price longed poignantly for freedom to rejoin him.

Two hours he roamed about the castle. The three girls, with their yellow *jambiyahs*, kept close behind him. And the wall of gigantic basalt blocks that skirted the flat mountain-top was forty feet high, guarded by other armed women in its studding towers. It appeared heart-breakingly impossible to leave Verl without Vekyra's permission.

Again, on the way back to his room, he met the sheikh Fouad el Akmet, walking intimately beside the yellow-branded girl.

Fouad nodded at her, and winked elaborately at Price. Brushing close as he passed, he whispered:

"Be at the east side of the central court, *Effendi*, at midnight."

The girl was beside him as he spoke; he ogled her, nudged her familiarly in the side. She smiled slyly back at him.

"You will be their, *Sidi?*"

Price nodded, and the old Bedouin grimaced craftily through his beard.

The girl, he suspected, was about to make a fool of the old Arab. And even if she were sincere, Price could not see how an escape was to be contrived. Surely not through the passages in the mountain, guarded by Malikar and his snake-men. And Price had seen no way to negotiate the half-mile precipices outside the walls. But he resolved to meet the old man—if he could get free of his own guards. No reason why he should not. And there was a chance. . . .

Vekyra came to his room that evening, a female slave behind her carrying the garments that Malikar had taken from him, and the oval golden buckler, the chain-mail, and the great ax that had been Iru's.

"These I made Malikar give me," she explained. "Do you wish to keep the ax?"

"Why, yes," Price said, puzzled, astonished, and delighted at this unexpected return of his possessions.

"Then promise me not to use it in Verl."

"I promise."

"The word of Iru is strong as the walls of Anz," she said. Then, smiling at him provocatively: "Iru, I would have you dine with me at sunset. The slaves will bring your garments."

And soon, declining the proffered aid of the armed girl, Price was donning a barbarically splendid outfit. *Kamis* of pure white silk, diaphanously thin. *Abba* of stiff, woven silver, lined with crimson silk, bordered with brilliant red. Something extraordinary, he thought, must be imminent.

When he was ready, the girls led him out of the room, down a long arcade whose twisted columns were alternately marble and gold, and into a long hall he had not seen before.

The high walls of burnished gold were inset with broad

panels of snowy alabaster, embellished with weird designs in black and crimson. On the walls flared silvery cressets, green and violet.

Day was already fading and the colored lights were dim; mysterious shadows lurked in the long hall. The air was surprizingly and deliciously cool; it bore a pungent hint of unfamiliar fragrance, as if incense were burning in the cressets.

The armed girls stopped at the curtained entrance. Price walked alone across the soft rugs to where Vekyra waited. For a moment he was self-conscious in the unfamiliar garments; the silver cloak felt stiff and heavy.

Two couches had been set in the farther end of the hall, broad and low, of some dark, antique wood, crimson-lacquered. Upon one Vekyra was reclining upon luxurious deep cushions. With feline grace she rose and came to meet Price and took his hands.

The sheath of scarlet about her pale-gold body made it almost white. A wide band of black about her head emphasized the ruddy splendor of her hair. She wore no jewels; her dress was richly simple. Perilous lights flamed in her Oriental eyes.

Silently she led him to one of the couches, and tried to pull him down beside her upon it. He drew quickly away, and seated himself opposite.

Angrily, she tossed her head.

"Listen, Vekyra," Price began abruptly. "I don't want to quarrel with you. But I want you to understand that I'm not trying to finish any old love story that started two thousand years ago. What I want——"

"Am I not beautiful?"

He looked at her. Slenderly curved and graceful, cased

in scarlet silk, she was beautiful. But her beauty was bright and cruel and terrible. "You are," he admitted.

"What do you want, Iru," she whispered, "that I can not give you?"

"See here, Vekyra, you don't understand——"

She cut him off with a petulant nod.

"What is it," she demanded in a voice that was soft, yet fierce, "that all men want the most? Love? Youth? Wealth? Power? Fame? Wisdom? Iru, I offer you not one, but all!"

"Oh, but don't you see——"

She shrugged impatient shoulders.

"You say I am beautiful. I give you a love that has lived through a hundred generations. A love that has brought you back from death, by its sheer living strength!"

Price started to speak, but saw that anything he said would only anger her. He listened in silence.

"Youth?" her silvery voice pealed the question. "When you and I are of the golden blood, you shall be young for ever. A few days in the yellow vapor—and your youth is immortal!"

Her slanted eyes burned.

"Wealth? Look around you. My castle is yours for the taking, and all the gold in the lair of the snake. Is that nothing?

"Fame? It is yours for the seeking, when you become the strongest of men, the wealthiest, and immortal.

"Wisdom? Care you nothing for the ancient secrets of Anz? I have the books of the wise men. The hall of illusion. The mirrors of gold. Many others. You spurn wisdom?"

"See here——" Price spoke again, and again she would not listen.

"And yet I offer you more. The thing men prize above all else. The thing they gladly trade all else for. What is that?

"Power! I give you the weapons of the ancient land. The command of the tiger, and the snake. Power to conquer all the world!"

She angrily clapped her small hands, and a slave-girl came into the room, carrying a red silken cushion upon which rested a crown of white metal, crusted with seed pearls, and set with large, primitively cut, red and yellow gems.

"The crown of Anz!" cried Vekyra. "It is yours, Iru. Once you wore it. I give it back to you."

She took the crown in her hands; the girl vanished silently.

Price gestured gravely. "I'm sorry, Vekyra, but you'll have to listen to reason. I don't say you aren't beautiful, for you are. And I understand you are offering me quite a lot. Probably some men would be glad enough to take you up."

She drew angrily erect, the coronet in her hands. Price waved her back to the couch.

"You might as well know the truth, even if it hurts. I love Aysa—no matter if you do say she is the reincarnation of a murderess. And I'm going to take her away from Malikar if it takes the rest of my life.

"If she is still human, well and good. And if she is already changed to gold, *then* will be time enough for me to think about going to sleep in that mist, myself.

"Sorry if it hurts. But it's better for you to know."

Vekyra had listened silently, breast heaving, tawny eyes flashing. She started to her feet again, and then sat back

219

down. Anger vanished from her face, like a discarded mask. She smiled obliquely at Price, with disarming, perilous sweetness.

"Iru, my lord," came her tinkling, honeyed tones, "let us not quarrel. The feast is ready."

Again she clapped, and serving-girls came through the curtained door. The platters they bore carried an astonishing variety of foods. Fresh dates. Scarlet, stoneless pomegranates. Huge purple grapes in clusters. Tiny, fragrant, hulled nuts, unfamiliar to Price. Roast meat. Spiced sweetcakes, of many shapes and flavors. Several varieties of cheese. A diversity of wines, in tall flagons, thin and sirupy-thick, sweet and sour, red and white and purple.

Price watched Vekyra, saw that she made a mere pretense of eating. She selected some morsel from each proffered platter; but those morsels seldom went to her mouth, she no more than sipped the wine. He wondered if she required ordinary food. Perhaps the golden beings needed only to breathe the yellow mist in order to live.

He resolved to eat and drink as sparingly as Vekyra. An intuitive feeling warned him that some crisis was approaching; he determined not to drug himself with food. Like her, he merely sipped and tasted, until the platters came no more.

He saw annoyed vexation in Vekyra's eyes, and was glad of his abstinence.

"Let us have music," she whispered, at length, and clapped again.

Soft strains welled up from hidden players, unfamiliar, oddly stirring. Low, dull, insistent, barbaric as jungle tom-toms.

"Now that you have dined"—and the tawny, oblique

eyes darted Price a malicious glance—"I shall dance for you."

She glided out upon a rug of dull blue and somber crimson and stopped there, swaying through the slow measures of an archaic dance. Through golden lashes her slanted eyes watched Price, mystic, enigmatic.

He forced his gaze away for a moment, tried to get a grip upon himself. He felt that a spell of evil was being deliberately woven about him.

It all seemed a play staged to influence him. The long, strange hall, dim in the colored, eldritch light of flaring cressets, filled with heady perfume. The weird, sobbing music, and Vekyra dancing, slim and elfish in her crimson tunic, red-golden hair loose like a net to snare him.

She began to sing a strange, simple song:

> *Red flames dance, jungle flames—dance and call.*
> *Drums throb deep, jungle drums—throb and call.*
> *Moon glows white, jungle moon—glows and calls.*
>
> *Swift heart throbs, heart of mine—throbs like drum.*
> *Hot blood flows, blood of mine—flows like flame.*
> *Passion glows, in my breast—glows like moon.*
>
> *Moon grows dim; red flames sink; drum is still.*
> *Yet I wait—ever wait—for my love.*
> *Ages pass; earth grows old—still I wait.*

Violet and green, the cressets flared, casting fantastic shadows upon gold and marble walls. Mysterious gloom filled the corners of the hall, and low music wailed, as Vekyra writhed and swayed and sang. The cool incense in the air was like a wine, intoxicating.

221

Golden Blood

The music quickened suddenly. Vekyra spun with it, light and graceful as a dancing flame. And as she danced she stripped the crimson tunic from her bright and splendid body, flung it down and whirled over it.

The music died to far-off, haunting strains, and she came toward Price. Nearly nude. Like a statue in pale gold, come to life and walking. Her tawny-greenish eyes were hot with passion.

She flung herself down beside Price, threw her bare arms around him. Desire rose in him instantly, like a burning wind. Involuntarily, he slipped an arm around her delicately molded shoulders, drew her throbbing body to him. She lifted a pale, oval face, oblique eyes wild, aflame with passionate exultation.

Price stared for a moment into her mad, greenish eyes, and felt a sudden horror of her. He turned his face away from her seeking lips, tried to push her from him. Her bare yellow arms clung to him with amazing strength. She drew him against her body, and called out.

A slave-girl ran into the room with a crystal bowl of purple wine.

"Drink, Lord Iru," Vekyra whispered, as Price struggled in her golden arms. "Drink and forget."

She clung to him, and the girl forced the wine against his lips.

He did not want to strike a woman . . . but she was not a woman, this golden vampire.

Snatching one arm free, he knocked the wine to the floor, where it spread like blood. Vekyra still clung to him, and he drove his fist at her painted lips.

222

She flung him back at the couch, and hell was in her eyes.

"You strike Vekyra?" she hissed. "Me? Vekyra? Queen of Anz and priestess of the snake?"

Price scrambled to his feet and strode toward the curtained entrance.

"Go!" she flared at him. "And ask no mercy of Vekyra, for yourself—or the wretched slave you love!"

Deliberately, Price paced the length of the hall. He was almost at the curtained entrance when Vekyra called after him:

"Iru! Stay, Lord Iru!"

He looked back, saw her running after him across the rich rugs, pale and beautiful in the dim, flaring lights of green and violet. He dropped the curtain, heard beyond it her choked cry of rage and hate.

As he hastened along the splendid arcade to his own apartment in the moonlit palace, Price quoted uncomfortably:

"Hell hath no fury like a woman scorned!"

26. VEKYRA'S VENGEANCE

EVEN THEN, Price was far from understanding the subtlety of Vekyra's nature. As he strode back to his room, escorted by the armed girls, and exchanged the resplendent ceremonial garments for his own clothing, he was expecting her destroying fury to fall upon him at any instant. He was certain that the infuriated woman would seek some revenge, but he failed to anticipate its nature.

The girls, with their *jambiyahs*, had retired to the doorway of his room. The change of clothing completed, he donned the linked yellow mail of Iru, and lay down on the bed with the ancient king's oval buckler and the golden ax beside him.

He did not sleep. At any instant he expected something to happen. Just what course Vekyra's revenge would take, he did not know. Would she come herself to murder him? Send the tiger in after him? Or merely return him to Malikar?

A full moon was shining, but the broad, unglazed windows of his room faced southwest; the silver light did not enter them. The guards in the doorway had a torch, but it flickered low, presently hissed and went out. Price listened to the girls. They talked, for a time, in low tones. Then their voices ceased. He heard deep breathing, as if some of them were sleeping.

Abruptly, he remembered his promise to meet the old sheikh at midnight, in the middle court. He had no great hope that anything would come of it. But at any rate it would be an interesting way to pass a few hours of the night. And if he *could* get outside the castle, free to use the golden ax again . . .

The girls in the doorway did not stir as he rose silently from the bed and crossed the dark room to the unglazed windows. Softly he glided over the sill, let himself down by his arms, and dropped quietly upon the gravel walk. There was no alarm; it was amazingly simple.

The castle was strangely bright. Moonlight reverberated from bright marble and polished gold. It filled the courts and colonnades with silent, ghostly splendor.

A man could not have hidden easily in that moonlight. But there seemed to be no one about. Price slipped along sleeping paths, until he reached the middle court. That, too, was empty, uncannily still in moon-drenched wonder.

He felt almost foolish for coming here at all; it was ridiculous to trust in the old Bedouin *nakhawilah* to plan his escape. Price was uncertain whether to return to his room or to make a suicidal attempt to scale the castle walls and climb down the precipices.

"You, *Effendi?*" whispered Fouad, from the shadows of a mass of shrubbery.

Price moved toward him. The old Arab came into the moonlight. He was armed with a long javelin. The woman who had been his guard was beside him, *jambiyah* at her waist and a coil of rope on her arm.

"*Wallah, Sidi,*" muttered the sheikh. "I am glad you came! A bad place this is, by moonlight. I like not the golden woman-*djinni.*"

"Come now, silently," murmured the girl.

225

She led the way along a shadowed arcade of palms to the eastern wall of the castle. Hanging down the basalt barrier was a rope ladder, just to northward of one of the towers that studded the wall.

"Up that," the girl whispered. "Make no sound. Wait in the shadow of the tower."

Price climbed up, Fouad after him. The girl followed, carrying her rope. They stood on the top of the wall, six feet wide. On one side was Verl, argent, glorious in the moonlight; on the other, a half-mile of sheer space, above lava plains that were grim desolation.

The girl fastened the end of her rope to the metal hooks that held the rope ladder, then dropped it over the outer face of the wall.

"Slip down, quickly," she hissed. "You will find a path, cut in the rock. No noise. And quickly, before the mistress awakes."

Fouad advanced upon the girl, as if to embrace her. She shrugged impatiently, pushed him toward the rope. He seized it, vanished over the wall. Price waited until it went slack.

He was troubled. This escape seemed too easy. Something was wrong, but just what, he could not guess.

He followed down the rope, letting it slip through his hands. Fouad's hands reached up and caught him, guided him to a narrow ledge. He released the rope. It was whisked swiftly upward.

The ledge sloped downward, to the right, a path two feet wide, cut in the rock. It was smooth; the granite projected out above it. Price hastened away along it, Fouad following.

Still he was worried about the escape. It had been too simple. But on one point he was relieved. He was outside the castle. His promise no longer held him from using the golden ax.

The path zigzagged back and forth across the east face of the mountain. Above a steep, smooth slope, they came to the end of it, and half climbed, half slid down to the lava plain.

Side by side, they ran away from the mountain.

"Wallah, Effendi," gasped Fouad. "We'll be in El Yerim by dawn."

When they were a mile away, Price looked back. The black mass of the mountain loomed behind them, grim and threatening. He saw the yellow square of the gates where he had once vainly demanded admission. Far above loomed the castle, a glowing opalescent coronal under the moon.

They went on, running. Price was afraid. Still he did not understand the escape. Something about it was not as it should be.

"Ya Allah!" Fouad screamed suddenly, when they were perhaps two miles across the lava flows, in the direction of the oasis. His voice was strained and distorted with fear.

He was looking back. Price turned, and scanned the ominous black pile of the mountain, across moon-flooded desert. The golden square had vanished. The tunnel-gates were open!

Then he saw the tiger, a golden monster, running across the lava fields, the *howdah* on its back. Already it had come half a mile. He could make out Vekyra's tiny figure upon the swaying beast.

He knew, then, why the escape had been so simple and easy. And he understood the subtle horror of Vekyra's vengeance. All this was her planning. A trap! Fouad had not impressed his jailer as much as he supposed; no wonder she had been impatient to start him down the rope.

All this had been planned, even before he had won Vekyra's wrath. She had spared him, for the moment, because she had the subtle snare of revenge already set and baited.

"Ya Allah! Ya gharati!" Fouad was howling. "The *djinni* but tricks us to hunt us again!"

His voice went hoarse and died in his beard. Over the desert, through the still golden rain of moonlight, wailed the ululant squall of the hunting tiger.

27. THE CAMP IN THE WADI

PRICE AND THE OLD BEDOUIN both ran when the golden tiger screamed. In the thin, uncanny ululation was some quality that shattered the nerves and woke blind, atavistic terrors. They were no longer reasoning beings. That squalling cry, with all that it meant, made them mere frightened animals.

Together they ran across the livid, moon-washed lava flows, nerved by fear to almost superhuman exertions. When Price came to himself, red pain seared his laboring lungs; every breath had become a sobbing gasp. Hot sweat drenched him; the night was suddenly oppressive; his limbs were stiff and leaden.

He made himself stop. The oasis was a dozen miles away; to reach it ahead of the tiger was an obvious impossibility. The mad flight was gaining him nothing; it was serving only to increase Vekyra's pleasure in her diabolically planned revenge.

Price dropped, panting, on his stomach behind a jagged knob of black lava. Fouad ran on, howling out at every leap a frantic appeal to Allah and his prophet.

From the shadow of the rock, Price looked back across the dark, barren, argent-lit plain, toward the mountain, watched the vague yellow form, appearing and dissolving in the ghostly light. Zor, the golden tiger; Vekyra riding on his trail.

He lay quiet, fondling the helve of the golden ax. It was madness, of course, to think of battling the elephantine tiger, but no more suicidal than flight; and he always felt better fighting than running.

229

He watched the tiger running with effortless strength, as if it floated upon the waves of white moonlight. It came straight toward him, then turned a little. He heard Vekyra's triumphant view-haloo, a pealing silver shout.

She had seen him. No. It must be Fouad. In the shadow of the rock, he must be yet invisible to her. But she would certainly discover him as she came nearer. And the great yellow cat, if it trailed by scent——

His thought was broken off by a sudden rattle of rifle-fire, from the direction Fouad had taken. Bullets hummed and whined above his head, singing toward the tiger.

The running beast stopped suddenly, stood motionless. It was not five hundred yards away. Price could see the *howdah,* and Vekyra sitting in it. She stood up, looked for a moment after Fouad, with the bullets whistling about her.

Then she crouched low; the tiger turned and fled. The yellow bulk of it paused for an instant upon a distant ridge; then it seemed to melt away in the moonlight.

Price got to his feet, swearing in astonished relief. The abrupt reaction to his extreme nervous tension of a few moments before made him feel curiously weak and shaken. He had an odd desire to laugh.

Cunning as Vekyra's plot had been, to raise the hopes of her victims by allowing them to make that miraculous escape, then to run them down upon the tiger, she had bungled it. She had actually given them the freedom with which she had planned to tantalize them.

Walking in the direction Fouad had fled, Price came soon in view of half a dozen men, rifles in hand, standing about

230

the old Arab. One of them challenged him; he shouted out his name, and old Sam Sorrows, the rangy Kansan, came hastening to meet him.

"Howdy, Mr. Durand," he called, surprized. And when he was nearer: "What's it all about, anyhow?"

"The lady on the tiger was out for a bit of sport. Hunting, with Fouad and me for the game. Lucky we ran into you."

"Maybe." Sam Sorrows lowered his voice to a whisper. "Better keep an eye peeled for that half-breed de Castro, Mr. Durand. The skunk hasn't actually loved you, ever since you took that girl out of his yellow hands. Say, have you found out anything——"

"Yes, Sam, I saw her. Down in the mountain. That golden devil, Malikar—he's turning *her* to gold. But about de Castro?"

"Well, he doesn't worship the ground you walk on. And the men are pretty well with him. And—well, you see— that is to say——"

The old man paused, doubtful, fumbling his Lebel in the moonlight.

"What is it, Sam?"

"Well, Mr. Durand, you see—anyhow, *we saw you yesterday, in the mirage.*"

"Oh!" Price recalled his weird experience in the hall of illusion. "What of it?"

"Well, sir, I don't like to say it. But it was plain to see you and the yellow woman were spying on us. Looked like she was on pretty good terms with you. The men were saying——"

"Saying what?" Price prompted him again.

231

"Of course *I* don't doubt you, Mr. Durand." Price was shocked to note the faintest uncertainty in the old man's tones, as if he were not quite convinced. "But the men think you've sold us out. De Castro was making some unpleasant remarks about what would happen if we got hold of you again. Thought I'd put you on guard."

"Thanks, Sam." Price squeezed his gnarled hand.

"You'll have to talk, sir. It looks queer, you happening to run into us this way, with the woman making out to chase you. The men will think you planned the thing, to get back in camp, and find out what we're planning."

"But Fouad was with me, too."

"What does he amount to?" The old Kansan turned back toward the others. "Good luck, sir. Remember, I'm *for* you."

In a shallow *wadi* beyond the ridge Price found a small, fireless camp. There were no tents. The white men, an even score of them, were mostly sprawled or squatting about the camel packs. Fouad's Arabs, now numbering a little over thirty, were gathered in a clamoring group about their new-returned sheikh. Close about were the dromedaries, kneeling or awkwardly sprawling. And the gray, silent bulk of the tank.

Jacob Garth came to meet Price, as Sam Sorrows walked with him past the little group of sentinels on the ridge. A huge, gross man, his fat head bared to the night breeze, his *topi* slung about his neck.

"Don't trust him too far," the lanky Kansan whispered again. "He'll do anything to humor de Castro and the men——till he gets the gold in his own fat hands!"

The man was near; Price did not reply.

"So *you're* back again, Durand?" boomed Garth's voice, sonorous and emotionless as ever.

"Yes."

"Doesn't it occur to you that you have been deserting and appearing again rather too often to be convincing?"

"I think not. I can explain."

"You can explain why we saw you in the mirage yesterday morning? And on evidently intimate terms with the golden woman—whom you now pretend to be running away from?"

"Yes."

"Go ahead."

"Listen, Garth. You may think me a traitor. I admit that I did have a chance—or rather two chances—to double-cross you. I was running from that tiger because I didn't do it. Garth, I've been pretty well through the mountain. I know a good deal, I imagine, that might be useful, if you are planning another attack on the mountain—I suppose you are?"

"So it's both ends against the middle, eh?"

Price flushed, struggled to control his voice.

"Garth, I have given you no reason to doubt my honor. I'll tell you honestly what I have learned about our enemies. But first I must have assurance that you—and your men— will respect my life and freedom."

Pale and icy in the moonlight, the man's eyes glittered at Price from the broad white mask of his pouchy face.

"Very well, Durand," he said at length. "I'll tell you this much: We are striking about sunrise. In a few minutes

Golden Blood

Sam Sorrows is riding back to El Yerim with orders for the planes. They're to bomb the castle. That will finish that accursed mirage?"

"If they can hit the machine. A complicated lot of mirrors and such in the dome of the highest tower."

"Good. Your information may be worth while, after all. With the planes, the tank, and the guns, we can smash any other opposition. We are going to dynamite our way into the mountain. You tell me what you know. Go over the plan with me. I'll promise you safety. But I'll want to keep you under guard until after the battle."

"One other thing——" began Price.

"You thinking about the girl? Well, Mr. Durand, you had better understand right now that I've promised her to de Castro, if we happen to come across her. You'll have to forget her."

"The injustice of the thing——"

"Justice isn't worrying me, Durand. Gold is what I'm after. Tell me your story, if you like, and I'll give you protection from the men. If you don't like it, I'll turn you over to de Castro. He'd like well enough to twist a knife in you. He's asleep. Shall I call him?"

Argument was in vain; Price as last submitted. He was still relating the tale of his adventures, and describing the interior passages of the mountain, when there was a sudden stir among the sentries on the ridge above the camp. A warning shot, a shouted challenge.

"Jacob Garth! Jacob Garth! Jacob Garth!"

A silver voice was pealing through the moonlight. Vekyra's voice. Price's heart thudded. What did this mean?

234

"Come along." Garth took his arm. They went back to the crest. Two hundred yards across the moon-bathed lava stood Vekyra, a vague figure, almost spectral in the argent light. She was on foot; the tiger was not visible.

"Is that *she?*" Garth asked Price.

"Yes. The golden woman. Name's Vekyra."

"What do you want?" Garth bellowed in Arabic.

The liquid voice floated back, "Jacob Garth! Jacob Garth!"

The big man hesitated. He looked back at the camp, and then peered around over the white-lit desert. His voice rolled out suddenly, calm, serene as always:

"I'm going out to talk to her. If anything goes wrong, shoot. And keep *him* here." He nodded at Price. "Take good care of him; he may be useful."

Jacob Garth strode out across the desert. The sentries stood ready on the hill, Price among them. They saw Garth stop as he came near the woman; heard a faint murmur of voices. The two presently moved a little farther away, and sat down on the ground, face to face.

It was nearly an hour later that they rose. The woman's ghostly form ran fleetly away, until it dissolved in the moonlight, reappeared, and was gone. Jacob Garth stalked deliberately back to the sentries. Though all of them must have been bursting with curiosity, none dared address him.

"Did you satisfy yourself about my status with the woman?" asked Price.

Garth looked at him, rumbled slowly. "Yes, Durand. You must have played the fool with *her*. Come here."

The man led him a little away from the sentries, lowered his voice:

235

"Durand, we won't be needing you any further. And I'm convinced, from what the woman tells me, that you won't—can't—do us any harm. You can go."

"Go?" asked Price, blankly.

"Get out of camp, as you came. And the quicker the better. Joao de Castro doesn't like you. And the woman doesn't. Better get out while you can."

He turned to the sentries, and boomed:

"Mr. Durand is leaving us, men. Give him ten minutes to get out of bullet range."

28. THE SENTINEL SERPENT

SORRY IT'S HAPPENING this way, Mr. Durand," grinned Sam Sorrows. "But it might have been worse."

He had gone down to his kneeling camel. He brought Price a small canteen full of water, stuffed his pockets with dates, dried camel-flesh and hardtack.

"That will see you back to the oasis, sir. And good luck."

Tears were almost in Price's eyes as he gripped the old Kansan's hand, and walked away beneath the rifles of the sentries.

Half a mile away, a lava ridge intervened, shut him from sight of camp and sentries. He strode moodily along, through the hostile lava-desert. He had fumbled everything; his last chance was gone.

But it was not in Price's nature to quit. He never seriously intended to go meekly back to the oasis. And now the desperate plan flashed suddenly into his mind.

He knew a way into the mountain—the way along which the unwilling snake-man, Kreor, had once guided him. He remembered it well enough to follow it alone. It might be guarded, now, but he could take the risk. And he still had the golden ax.

Within the mountain were perils that he did not like to contemplate. The fanatic acolytes of Malikar. The insidious golden man himself. The yellow snake, that he would have to pass to reach Aysa—he shuddered again at memory of the cold, ancient evil that burned hypnotic in the serpent's eyes.

237

Most of all, he dreaded the aureate mist. The sinister sleep of the golden vapor had overwhelmed him on the other occasion. Even if he escaped all the other dangers, he would not have time to reach Aysa and carry her above it before it overcame him.

But perhaps he could devise some sort of protection! A rude gas mask. He ransacked his knowledge of such things. The masks used against first German attacks, at Ypres, he recalled, were mere dampened cloths. A wet cloth would be worth trying, at any rate. If the yellow gas united with or replaced the water in the human body, it must have a special affinity for it.

Filled with new hope that ignored the overwhelming chances against success, he hastened westward, circled around the west side of the mountain. Weary after a strenuous night, he flung himself down when he reached the point where Kreor and he had begun the climb up the sheer north precipice, and rested the hour until dawn, though he dared not sleep.

Sunrise found him toiling painfully and perilously up the cliff. Droning of airplane motors reached his ears, then thuds of heavy explosions that seemed to come to him through the very rock of the mountain.

Garth, then, had attacked; with Vekyra, probably, as an ally. Price's heart sank at a vision of what would happen, in that case, if they reached the place of the snake ahead of him. Aysa, hated as she was by Vekyra, might meet a fate worse than Joao's embrace.

At last he reached the fissure, slipped through into the dark, winding caverns of the mountain. Soon he was beyond all light, with nothing to guide him save memory. Many times he stumbled painfully against sharp-edged stone. But at last he came into the larger cavern, and through it, into the first hewn passage.

Onward, he found his way with comparative ease, counting his paces, turning as he and Kreor had turned. He came finally into the sloping, spiral way, and hastened downward, still through utter darkness.

Again the mass of the mountain quivered to an explosion. Then, for a few moments, he heard confused shouting, and the distant rattle of small arms, borne to him down some corridor.

He had expected to meet watchmen. But perhaps the entire forces of Malikar had been drawn to some other part of the passage, to oppose the entrance of Jacob Garth and Vekyra. And, as he was to discover, Malikar had left a sentinel more terrible than any human.

Sounds of fighting ceased, and he came finally into air that was suffused with the faintest possible yellow light. Steadily it grew brighter as he descended, until he passed the end of the passage leading to the gallery from which he first had seen the lair of the snake.

There the light of dancing golden atoms was strong in the air, the walls of the passage all a-glitter with rime of yellow crystals.

The passage flattened, straightened, and he came once more into the vast temple hall. The wonder of it smote him again. Circular, high-domed room, thick with shimmering yellow vapor, its black stone walls crusted with gold.

A furious hissing roar greeted him as he ran out upon the vast floor that lay between the entrance and the narrow bridge that spanned the giddy, green-golden abyss.

Leaping back in alarm, he saw the golden snake, coiled between him and the bridge that was the way to Aysa.

The reptile's thick coils were gathered in a conical heap. Every scale shone xanthic yellow, glittering, metallic. The tapering gold column of its neck was lifted. Ten feet above the floor, its vast flat head swayed back and forth as it hissed.

Price stared for a moment, fascinated again by those terrible eyes. The ugly head was gold-hooded, triangular. The vast, yellow-fanged mouth yawned wide as it hissed with such startling volume of sound.

The eyes transfixed him. Dreadful eyes. Purple-black, glowing with strange fire. Hard and fascinating as giant gems. Price found himself unconsciously responding with his own body to the swaying of the eyes, felt the chill of them stealing into his body, freezing his limbs, choking him, oppressing his breathing, slowing his heart.

Desperately he fought against the power of the snake. Once, when the reptile appeared in the mirage, he had broken free. He could again! And he had seen Malikar overcome the snake, whip it into submission. The serpent itself was not immune to fear.

Calling upon every atom of his will to lift each foot, Price walked stiffly, unsteadily, like a mechanical doll, directly toward the snake. Awkwardly, he raised the yellow ax, with numb and nerveless hands. Malikar, he remembered suddenly, had shouted at the snake.

Price found his throat dry, his voice a hoarse croaking. But he began gasping out the ax-song of Iru, in short, harsh phrases.

The undulatory motion of the flat head ceased. It drew back, and, still hissing, struck at him. Price called upon flagging muscles to fling up the oval buckler to guard his face.

But the yellow head did not quite reach him. The snake was afraid. It drew back again, its movement doubtful, frightened.

The chill of strange fascination thawed from Price's body. Shouting the ax-song louder, he continued his deliberate advance.

The wedge-shaped head drew back. It sank upon the coils, lay motionless. Purple-black eyes glittered at Price, alien, hostile—yet afraid.

Still he moved forward, fighting down, striving to conceal the naked terror of his revolting soul.

His legs came against the cold, smooth scales of its outermost coil. The flat head, yellow-hooded, was sunk down before him, strange eyes watching him with glittering intentness, evilly aflame with supernormal intelligence, terrible with wisdom older than men.

Shuddering, Price slapped the frightful head, as he had seen Malikar do, with his open hand. He was sick with fear, weak, trembling. Every fiber of his body shrank trembling from contact with the snake. But he was afraid *not* to strike it.

The thick body against his legs shook a little, but the great head, the sinister, glittering eyes, did not move.

241

Golden Blood

With open hand he struck the cold, metal-scaled head a dozen times, so hard that his fingers stung, still shouting out the ax-song.

Then he turned away, forcing himself to move deliberately, not daring to look back. He walked to the end of the narrow bridge, and set foot upon the giddy way across the cavernous abyss to the niche where he had found Aysa, sleeping.

29. GOLDEN BLOOD

ODDLY, Price felt no vertigo, nor any fear of falling, as he started once more across that dizzy span, through thick, shimmering mist of gold. A single arch of black, gold-crusted rock, springing sheer across the yellow-green, infinite void, its unrailed path not two feet wide. In his concern for the sleeping girl, he was unconscious of any danger.

In the exigencies of his uncanny struggle with the serpent, he had even forgotten the soporific influence of the yellow vapor. He was midway across the abyss before it was recalled to him by sudden and overpowering lassitude, by a dullness of brain and a heaviness of limb.

He held his breath to run the remaining hundred feet to the great niche, with its four slabs of gold-rimmed rock, for he dared not stop above the abyss. Safely upon the shelf, he fumbled for his handkerchief, wet it from the canteen old Sam Sorrows had provided, and knotted it about his head, so that it covered his nose and mouth.

Aysa still lay upon the slab. Again he saw her lovely face, a-glitter with powder of gold. Still she was sunk in deepest sleep, breathing regularly, very slowly. Fearfully he brushed her cheeks and forehead, her small hands—and voiced a shout of pure joy! Beneath yellow dust, her hands and face were softly pliant, naturally white. The dread change had not yet taken place. It must require months, perhaps even years.

He tried to wake the girl. Utterly limp, completely relaxed, she did not rouse when he shook her, nor respond to his calling of her name.

Then a rushing sibilance roared through the temple. The snake, coiled before the entrance to the Cyclopean hall, was hissing angrily again. And Vekyra was riding toward it, upon the golden tiger.

Hissing savagely, the gigantic yellow reptile threw itself toward the invaders. Vekyra flung herself nimbly from the *howdah* and ran to meet it, while the tiger crouched, snarling ferally.

The rich voice of the golden woman pealed out in strange, melodious syllables. Fearlessly she approached the hissing snake. It did not strike, but coiled again before her, lowering its lifted head.

She stood a while before it, her voice still ringing out, and at last it thrust its head toward her. She advanced again, caressed it, slipped her yellow arms around the great column of the neck. Her voice sank to a whisper.

Abruptly she turned, left the reptile coiled quietly. The tiger was still snarling uneasily; she silenced it with a shouted word. It sank back upon its haunches, watching the motionless snake.

Drawing from her tunic a flashing golden blade, narrow and keen as a stiletto, she ran past the snake and started swiftly across the narrow bridge. Then Price knew that she had come to murder Aysa.

Snatching up the golden ax, Price hastened out upon the bridge to meet her. He knew that her passion for him had turned to hatred. He would have to fight for his own life, as well as Aysa's.

The gloating triumph upon Vekyra's painted yellow face gave way to stunned surprize. And surprize became sinister elation.

They met a hundred feet out upon the gold-frosted bridge. Vekyra stopped a dozen feet in front of him, greeted him with a mocking smile, her tawny-green, oblique eyes flashing maliciously.

"Peace upon you, Iru," she greeted him, her silky voice taunting. "Peace—if you wish it!"

"And on you, peace," Price replied solemnly, "if you will depart."

"*Lah!* But Iru, have you yet changed your mind?" She spoke mockingly. "You know that I talked with Jacob Garth last night. I promised him all that I promised you. He accepted; together we entered the mountain. He is even now fighting Malikar, in the halls above. I broke past, and came here to cut this wretched slave-girl into pieces and throw her into the abyss, where she can make no more trouble."

Price cursed her.

She smiled at him, enigmatically. "Yet, Iru, have you changed your mind? Will you forget the slave, and accept the crown of Anz?"

"Nothing doing!" snapped Price. "Get out—or fight!"

Vekyra laughed. With her rapier-like golden blade she pointed at the shining chasm below. Involuntarily, Price looked down into the illimitable gulf; his head swam with the sheer vastness of the pit beneath the giddy bridge.

"Then you and your precious slave-girl shall be for ever together," she taunted, "—*there!*"

Lightly she darted forward, yellow blade hissing.

Price met her point with the golden buckler, and swung the ancient ax. Vekyra leapt backward easily; and the force of his swing with the heavy ax almost toppled Price from the bridge.

As he struggled desperately to regain his balance, the yellow woman leapt forward again, her sword flashing at his throat. Price had to give ground to save himself, and one foot went half off the bridge.

Vekyra laughed at the sudden despair he could not keep from his face.

"Remember, Iru, the golden folk can not die!" she mocked. "And you are a mortal—though you may be born again for me to slay!"

Once more she slipped in, thrust, and repeated, with baffling swiftness. The ancient mail turned her stroke. But it was becoming evident to Price that he had met a very formidable opponent.

His shirt of mail and oval buckler gave him an advantage that was apparent only, for their weight slowed him, made it more difficult to keep his balance. And he could not swing the great ax effectively, lest the force of his own blow carry him off the bridge.

Vekyra, seemingly gifted with a perfect sense of balance, danced back and forth upon the gold-rimmed rock, thrusting, lightning-swift, with her narrow blade, easily avoiding his own awkward blows.

Again and again Price was forced to step perilously backward along the narrow way. He half regretted the impulse that had carried him out upon the dizzy arch; yet he dared not have Vekyra with him upon the ledge beyond, lest she slip past him and stab the sleeping girl.

He determined to try to reach the end of the bridge, where he would have ample footing, and might still keep Vekyra upon the narrow path.

Fending off a score of lightning strokes, as he precariously retreated, he found himself at last upon the edge of the shelf.

A golden witch, Vekyra still danced upon the bridge. And here he could swing the massive ax without fear of its weight carrying him off into the awesome, yellow-green chasm.

Vekyra thrust once more, her yellow blade reaching for his throat. Tightening his grip upon the ax-helve, Price swung furiously.

The ax bit into her shoulder. Her sword-arm went limp. The blade fell from it, clattered on the lip of the abyss, and fell silently into the green-gold flame.

With a choking cry of rage and hatred, Vekyra leapt backward on the narrow path, pressing a pale hand to her wound. It was not deep, but blood sprang from it, fell in little glistening gouts upon the bridge. Golden blood. It was yellow and it gleamed like molten metal.

She stood a few moments there on the bridge, glaring at Price with baleful flames in her oblique, tawny eyes. Then, springing with the silent ferocity of a tigress, she leapt forward to attack him with naked golden hands.

Price stood grimly guarding the end of the bridge, with Iru's ax uplifted. He tried to strike at Vekyra, as she lunged

at him, and he found that he could not. Some deep, blind force in him rebelled at hewing down an unarmed woman— even such a woman as Vekyra.

Dropping the ax behind him, he drove his fist at the golden witch. With incredible agility she avoided the blow, and flung herself upon him. She had recovered the use of the arm momentarily paralyzed by the wound.

Price instantly regretted the blind, instinctive chivalry that had made him discard the ax. She was no woman, this golden witch! Like a tigress she hurled herself upon him, clawing at him with yellow talons, slashing at him with her teeth.

Beneath her rush he stumbled, and they fell together on the gold frost at the lip of the abyss.

For a few moments they rolled and twisted in furious struggling on the floor. The golden woman was super-normally strong; she fought with savage, demoniac energy. Then they staggered back to their feet, still locked in a straining embrace.

Price knew a little of wrestling, but not enough to cope with her maniacal strength. He was wet with sweat; his panting breath hissed through the rag tied over his face, and he felt that one thing was smothering him. His body ached with intolerable weariness.

Vekyra was panting, too, her swift breath puffing upon him. Her hot body was slippery with her own golden blood. But again and yet again she eluded his holds, while her own yellow arms held him in an unbreakable grasp.

Slowly, inexorably, she forced him toward the brink of the abyss. Then he tripped her, and they fell again. The sharp lip of the pit bit into his shoulder. His head was over the edge. He had a momentary glimpse of shining, golden-green depths.

Instinctively his grasp upon the golden body tightened. If he went into the abyss, it would not be alone.

The yellow woman screamed, struggled desperately to free herself. Together, they toppled slowly over the chasm's lip. Vekyra released him, made a last, frantic effort to save herself.

Certain she could reach no support, Price freed his own hands and snatched desperately at the edge of the precipice. His fingers closed upon the sharp edge of the rock, and an instant later his weight came upon them, straining weary muscles until they cracked.

The golden woman fell free of him. A single shriek of agonized terror floated upward, as she was swallowed in the golden-green vapor of the pit.

Mutely thankful that he, and not Vekyra, had been next the lip of rock, and hence able to grasp it in that last frantic instant, Price hung precariously by his arms. Slowly, with infinite effort, he inched his way up, flung his body over the edge of the black rock, and drew himself shakily to safety.

As he stood up, panting and trembling, he heard the crashing of guns and the clatter and roar of the tank. Peering through the golden mist above the abyss, he saw a little group of blue-robed snake-men, making a stubbornly fought retreat into the great hall, before blazing rifles.

30. GOLD AND IRON

WITH A SICK HEART, Price watched the battle across the abyss. The result of it meant little to him. If the snake-men won, he and Aysa would be again at the mercy of Malikar. If the invaders should be the victors, they would share no better at the hands of Joao de Castro and the others.

No more than a dwindling handful, the blue priests stood just at the entrance, savagely contesting the advance with pike and spear. Then the gray bulk of the tank roared through them, its guns beating their march of death.

The snake-men—the few that survived—scattered wildly across the broad, gold-frosted floor. But the invaders were not yet victorious. The giant snake, hissing again, flung forward from where Vekyra had left it.

The tank stopped abruptly, and the little group of white men behind it. Price saw the yellow reptile's head swaying back and forth, knew that the men must be experiencing the deadly fascination of its terrible eyes.

Tearing his gaze away from the battle, Price turned to Aysa, tried again to wake her. His improvised gas mask was evidently protecting him from the somniferous influence of the golden vapor. Perhaps the girl would recover, if he fixed one for her. They might at least have a few minutes together, before the finish.

He removed her *kafiyeh,* shook the yellow, metallic powder from it, drenched it with water and spread it over her quiet face. He was wetting his own handkerchief again when a startling chorus of furious growls and hisses drew his attention back across the pit.

250

The golden tiger had attacked the snake. The two monstrous beings thrashed about the frosted floor in colossal combat. The tiger, bulky as an elephant, and stronger, still carrying the black *howdah,* was slashing ferociously at the reptile with claw and fang.

It found the snake no mean opponent. As Price watched, the serpent whipped a gleaming yellow coil about the tiger's thick body, then another, and a third, constricting with crushing force. Still hissing, it struck with yellow fangs.

A Titan conflict of semi-metal giants, each preternaturally strong and powerful, each centuries old. The puny men beyond, dwarfed by this spectacle, stopped for a time to stare at the battle royal.

Then the tank came to lumbering life again. It clattered out upon the vast floor. Stuttering machine-guns moved back and forth, and the last of the snake-men, staring dazedly at this gigantic battle of their gods, fell upon xanthic frost.

Beast and reptile seemed evenly matched; Price's former allies, for the moment, were masters of the situation. He saw them gathered about the tank—but pigmies in this colossal place. Thick, gross Jacob Garth. Joao de Castro, small, alert, active. Huge, ape-like Pasic, the Montenegrin. A dozen others.

Sam Sorrows, Price's staunch friend, who might have aided him again, was not with them. Sam, he recalled, had returned to the oasis with orders for the planes. Muller was now driver of the tank.

Garth and Joao de Castro appeared to be arguing with Muller, who was looking through the manhole. The man shrugged, and retired into the machine. The motor

251

roared again, and the tank lumbered on through the yellow fog.

The Cyclopean battle was still at issue. The coils of the snake were constricting ever tighter about the tiger's body. The reptile had ceased to hiss; but golden fangs still flashed.

The tiger, far from conquered, was tumbling upon the gold-powdered floor, tearing desperately at the serpent's coils with savage claws. The glistening, metal-scaled body of the snake was ripped in many places, oozing bright, golden blood.

The tiger, evidently alarmed as the tank roared at them, staggered to its feet, lifting the squeezing snake clear of the floor. But the tank struck before it could leap aside. The force of the collision sent it reeling and staggering toward the abyss. It fell again, the inexorable coils of the serpent constricting ever tighter.

Perilously near the brink of the abyss the tiger had fallen. And seemingly it realized the danger, for, abandoning its attempts to rid itself of the snake, it struggled laboriously to its feet again, already half dead from the pressure of golden coils.

The tank's motor had stalled. For a little time the gray fighting-machine was motionless; then it roared into life again. The snake-burdened tiger was just heaving to its feet when the tank struck it. The impact sent it staggering once more toward the chasm's lip. The tank paused, roared after it.

It may be that the driver momentarily lost control of the tank, or perhaps he had not seen the abyss. At any rate, tank, tiger and snake went over the brink as one mass. Price watched them, falling free into the green-gold void, turning slowly about, the tiger still squeezed in an embrace of death. Yellow vapor hid them . . .

The roar of the madly racing motor died away below, and Price looked back across the abyss.

His former allies were victorious, masters at last of the treasure for which they had struggled so long. He faintly heard their feverish voices, saw them falling upon their knees, scraping up the thick encrustation of golden crystals from the floor with bare hands.

He watched Joao de Castro and Pasic toil madly to fill a little cloth sack, in which they had carried food, with the yellow dust. When it was full, both laid hands upon it. Pasic snatched it easily away; the Eurasian flung himself upon him, knife flashing. They struggled, and the gold spilled unnoticed on the yellow floor. Deliberately Jacob Garth drew out his automatic and shot them down in cold brutality.

Insane with the gold-lust, the others paid no heed. They remained scraping at the xanthic dust, until the sinister sleep of the golden vapor fell upon them. Jacob Garth took alarm at last, staggered toward the entrance with a hoarse cry of warning. But too late. . . .

No, the men had not won mastery of the gold—it had conquered them. They lay sprawled where they had fallen, motionless in the sleep that would endure until they were men of gold.

When Price realized all this meant, his heart skipped a beat with incredulous relief. The way was cleared, now, for him to carry Aysa out. When she was safe, he could return and give these men what aid he could. But the hope of his glorious moment was rudely shattered.

Malikar came striding into the enormous room, grim, diabolical giant in his crimson robes, a spiked golden mace upon his shoulder. With a caution worthy of his antiquity, he had kept clear of his enemies until they were helplessly sleeping.

One by one, he visited the inert men. Ruthlessly, methodically, he changed their slumber into one that would not end. He stood among them, then, for a little time, leaning upon the great mace—it was now no longer yellow, but encrimsoned with blood and brains—a golden Nemesis, red-robed.

Then, shouldering the reddened mace, he started across the bridge.

31. KISMET

IT HAD BEEN a tactical error to meet Vekyra upon the bridge, Price realized, because she had been quicker and more agile than himself. But, in Malikar's case, the same arguments did not apply. Vekyra had proved amazingly strong; Malikar's far bulkier body was doubtless far stronger. In a contest merely of strength, Price could be certain of defeat; he must make it a battle of skill. And skill, quickness, would count for far more upon the giddy span.

Black premonition of doom was in his heart. Three times before he had encountered Malikar; three times he had been bested.

He bent, brushed the golden frost from Aysa's lips with his own. A few moments before he had seen himself carrying the girl into sunlight and the open air, where she would surely wake. Now his brief cup of joy was shattered. Malikar, his other enemies gone, was more dangerous than ever.

A roar of startled rage told Price that Malikar had seen him. Brandishing the bloody mace, the giant came at a run. Replacing the damp cloth over the girl's face, Price snatched up the ancient ax.

Upon recognizing him, Malikar stopped. Resting the great club carelessly upon the narrow path, he laughed with a bellow of triumphant evil.

"Iru, again?" he shouted. "Fool, know you not that I am a god who can never die?"

"No, I don't," retorted Price, advancing.

"You can never conquer *kismet!*" The yellow priest chuckled thickly, with evil in his shallow eyes. "Three times we have met. And three times has fate struck you down.

"In the catacombs of Anz, *kismet* willed that your ax-helve should break. When we fought in the *wadi*, fate placed a loose stone beneath your foot. Again we met here, and *kismet* sent sleep upon you.

"You fight not *me* alone. *Kismet* is against you!"

Realizing that Malikar meant the boast merely as an attack upon his morale, Price ran forward to begin the battle, but the priest's mocking words had already served their purpose. They had filled him with the disturbing idea that all this adventure had been but a play of unseen forces, of sporting gods handling puppet strings, the idea that he was but a toy of cruelly jesting fate.

At his approach Malikar lifted the bloody mace, whirled it aloft and down. Oval buckler lifted, Price took the blow. It drove the shield down upon his head with stunning force, numbed his arms and shoulder.

An instant he reeled. The green-golden depths beneath the narrow bridge whirled confusingly. He made a desperate effort to clear his brain.

Korlu, the ancient ax, was lifted. And Malikar had not yet recovered the mace from his terrific blow. Price put every atom of his strength into a swing for the priest's red skull-cap.

Malikar ducked, but the hewing blade caught his shoulder.

The blow went true; it would have split an ordinary man to the abdomen. But Malikar was semi-metal. His skin was gashed, and bright yellow blood oozed out, but the wound was insignificant.

The violence of his own blow sent Price half off the bridge. He staggered awkwardly to regain his balance, as Malikar swung up the spiked club for another blow.

Price regained his balance, stepped backward and let the mace go past. As the force of his swing swayed Malikar toward the edge of the bridge, Price struck swiftly with the ax, in the hope of upsetting his balance. Malikar recovered easily, and evaded the ax.

Price struggled against grim despair. Human muscle and bone could not endure many such terrific blows as he had received; and the ax, swung true with his full strength behind it, had not seriously wounded the golden man. In any mere exchange of blows, Price knew, he was doomed. He had but a single chance of victory—to catch Malikar in a critical position, knock him off the bridge into the yawning abyss. And the priest appeared to possess caution and a cat-like sense of equilibrium.

Perforce, Price changed his tactics. No more did he come to close quarters. He kept his distance, tempting Malikar to strike, avoiding—when he could—the smashing mace, waiting for the moment when a quick blow might send the priest into the abyss.

The yellow giant pressed forward continually, so that Price was forced to give ground before each blow, retreating at grave risk of missing his footing on the dizzy way. Moreover, each step back brought Price nearer the niche where Aysa lay, lessening his chance of victory. For, once Malikar gained the platform, the battle would be lost.

257

Twice again the ax went home. It was splashed with golden blood; but Malikar seemed not inconvenienced by his wounds.

Price was reeling. Again and again the mace had fallen upon his buckler, despite his efforts to avoid it. His left arm and shoulder ached from the terrific shocks. His head rang from concussion, oppressed with mists of pain.

Exhaustion was near. The accumulated fatigue of many hours descended upon him. His present exertions were anything but light—lunging forward to draw the bloody mace, darting back to avoid it, swinging the yellow ax when opportunity presented.

Price dared not look back to see how much of the bridge remained behind him. But presently he glimpsed beneath his feet the glittering gouts of golden blood Vekyra had shed. Then he knew it was only a few feet to the platform, where he would be at Malikar's mercy.

Desperately he stood his ground, as the mace rose and fell again. It drove the lifted buckler down upon his head with staggering force. The ancient ax went out again, at Malikar's thick neck, all Price's strength behind it.

Fatigue and the faintness of concussion slowed his arm. Malikar swayed back. The yellow blade flashed futilely in front of his throat.

Half dazed as he was, Price staggered toward the edge of the bridge, drawn by the weight of his ax. He swayed for a moment over the side of the narrow span, while the green-golden void beneath spun crazily.

Before he could recover his balance, Malikar struck again

with the spiked golden club. Though his blow was hasty and relatively weak, its impact was staggering.

It struck Price's right shoulder. Painful numbness ran along his arm. His fingers, paralyzed, relaxed their grip upon the helve of the outflung ax. The golden weapon spun away from him, whirled silently into yellow-green mist.

Price's dazed mind reeled under the impact of the disaster as if from a second blow. Once more fate had stepped in, to defeat him.

"Kismet!" shouted Malikar, leering triumphantly.

He lumbered forward, his spiked mace lifted. Helpless, Price tottered uncertainly back, fighting to keep his head clear enough to stand upon the narrow way.

The bright pool of Vekyra's blood was just before Malikar, gleaming like a gout of molten gold. As he sprang forward, *kismet* once more entered the battle.

He stepped into the golden woman's blood. As if Vekyra's own malicious hand had seized his ankle, his foot slipped. He lurched forward awkwardly, shifting his heavy mace aside to maintain his balance.

Thus was provided the opening Price had been hopelessly fighting for. His whole body numb with fatigue and pain, he braced himself, swung his fist at the golden priest's head.

Into that blow went the last, convulsive effort of his tortured body. As he felt his fist meet solid flesh and bone, bright, glittering lights flashed up through the green-gold void, and darkness drowned them.

He fell flat upon the narrow bridge, flinging out his hands to clutch the xanthic-frosted rocks.

259

32. THE ANCIENT AYSA

M'ALME! M'ALME!"

The sweet, familiar voice came to Price's ears upon silver wings, through dull clouds of pain. Delicate hands were plastering a cold wet cloth upon his brow. Memory was gone; his mind, like his body, was bruised, stiff, inert.

"Master! Master!" the urgent voice kept pleading, in Arabic.

With a vague, dim impression that grave emergency, disaster, had been looming over him, Price forced open his eyes.

He lay upon a broad ledge of stone, frosted queerly with bright yellow crystals. He was propped against a huge slab of basalt. Before him was a bottomless pit of green-golden light, spanned with a bridge fantastically narrow. The world was thickly filled with dancing aureate mist—that mist, he remembered faintly, was somehow threatening.

Kneeling beside him was a girl. He turned his head painfully and looked at her. A lovely girl. Her hair was brown and waving, her skin a smooth, warm olive. Full, delicate, her mouth was pomegranate-red.

Wonderful, her eyes were. Somehow, they made him feel that he knew them. They were violet-blue, deep, mysterious, beneath long lashes. Keen pity was now in their shadowed depths, and distress.

Like the rocks about them, the girl's clothing glittered with xanthic frost. Smudges of yellow powder sparkled on her face and arms.

And she had been urgently calling to him in Arabic,

addressing him as "Master." Surely he could have no claim
upon a being so lovely! But if he did, the circumstance
was singularly fortunate.

He closed his eyes, racking his memory. This weird
place of golden vapors, outrageously fantastic as it might be,
was vaguely familiar. And he was certain he had known
the girl before, somewhere. Sight of her filled him with
a warming glow of pleasure.

He knew her name. It was—he probed dull mists of
weary pain—it was Aysa!

Aysa! His lips had muttered it aloud. At the sound, the
girl uttered a glad cry. She dropped beside him; her
arms went round him. Queer how pleasant her embrace
was! A delightful girl. He liked to have her near him; he
mustn't let her leave him, ever again. The nearness of
her filled him with quick, tingling joy.

It was good to lie here with her arms around him. But
he mustn't do that. There was some danger. . . . The
yellow mist. . . . He struggled with the idea: golden mist . . .
that was it; the mist turned people to gold. It would turn
him and Aysa into golden things. And he didn't want that to
happen.

He fumbled for the wet cloth the girl had been applying
to his forehead, made her tie it over her face. She understood quickly, fixed another for him. His arms ached when
he moved . . . he must have been fighting, to feel so
bruised and groggy. . . . Yes, he remembered hitting a
yellow man.

He inhaled through the damp rag and closed his eyes and
pondered the memory of the yellow man . . . a golden giant

of a man, in scarlet. . . . He must remember his name . . . Malikar! He would ask the girl about him; he spoke Arabic.

"Where is Malikar?" he whispered.

She pointed into the shining chasm.

"I woke, *m'alme*, with a wet cloth upon my face, and saw you fighting. Malikar struck you with his club. Then you hit him with your hand, and he stumbled into the pit. You fell upon the bridge, and I carried you back here."

His head was clearing now, since he was breathing through the cloth.

"But how did you come here so soon, *m'alme*, from Anz? It was just last night that Malikar locked you in the tomb of Iru, and told me you were dead."

Strange wonder was in the violet eyes.

Understanding swept through his brain, drove back the dull mists of oblivion. Everything was clear, now. And Aysa was with him, awake and free. Darling Aysa, for whom he had fought so long. It was not last night he had been locked in the catacombs of Anz, but many nights ago. But no need to tell her now.

He slipped one aching arm around her shoulders. She snuggled up contentedly against him, lifted violet eyes, shining with gladness. . . .

They must not stay here. The sleep of the golden vapor might steal upon them, unawares, with its strange transmutation. Aysa was not yet changed. But they must go, while they could. . . .

"You are tired, *M'alme*," Aysa whispered. "Let us rest here."

Jack Williamson

The sun was low, and the black, basaltic mass of *Hajar Jehannum* was three miles behind them, across smooth lava flows, the gold and alabaster of the palace of Verl glowing luridly in red sunset. Two hours ago they had come through the explosion-twisted yellow gates, where Jacob Garth had entered, and begun the long trek to the oasis.

"You must not call me master," Price told her, as they sat munching the hardtack and dried meat and dates old Sam Sorrows had given him.

"Why not? Am I not yours? And did you not once buy me for half my weight in gold?" She laughed. "And do I want anything save to be yours?"

"What do you mean, darling? Buying you?"

"You don't remember? The story of Aysa and Iru in old Anz? But you never heard it? I must tell you."

"Then there *was* a woman named Aysa in Anz, when Iru was king?"

"Of course, *m'alme*. I am named for her, because my eyes are blue, as hers were. Few, you know, among the Beni Anz, have blue eyes. The ancient Aysa was a slave; Iru bought her from the north country."

Price felt oddly disturbed. Was Vekyra's strange tale, after all, true? Was Aysa—his lovely, innocent Aysa—the namesake, if not the avatar, of a murderess?

"Well, don't worry about it, sweetheart!" Price told her. He put a bruised, stiff arm about her slender shoulders and drew her firmly to him. She laughed, a little, childish, happy laugh, and her violet eyes looked shining up at him.

He wasn't going to let anything take her away from him,

ever. No part of her. He was going to forget that silly story of Vekyra's. He didn't believe in this reincarnation business, anyhow . . . not too much. . . .

"I'll tell you the story, *m'alme*," Aysa whispered, in his arms.

"No, let's forget it. Nothing to it, anyhow. And happy as we are, we can't let anything——"

"But, *m'alme,* this story can not ruin our happiness."

"Then tell me, of course."

"Since he was a child, Iru the king was betrothed, by the wishes of his mother, to Vekyra, who was the daughter of a powerful prince—and not golden, then.

"Iru, by the legend, loved the slave-girl, Aysa. And Vekyra was jealous. One night she made the king drunk, and won the slave from him in a game of chance."

"I understand how she might have done that," said Price, recalling his own adventure in the castle of Verl.

"When Iru was sober, he demanded that Vekyra trade him back the slave. She dared not deny him. But she set the greatest price she could think of. She told Iru she would exchange him the girl for a tiger tame enough to ride.

"So Iru rode into the mountains, and caught a live tiger cub, and tamed it. When it was grown, he gave it to Vekyra, and she had to surrender the slave—but still she hated Aysa."

Price's disquiet was returning. This was the same story Vekyra had told, of the pampered and adored slave—who was to murder her adorer. He resisted an impulse to stop the girl. After all, what happened twenty centuries ago could not come between them now.

"Iru did not like the worship of the snake. He destroyed the snake's temple, slew its priests in battle. But Malikar, when all thought him dead, came back, a man of gold, to avenge the desecration of the temple. In vain he made war on Iru, and at last he disguised himself and slipped into Anz, to slay Iru by stealth.

"He found a woman to do murder for him."

Price's heart sank. This was the same evil tale.

"I know not what he told Vekyra. He must have offered her the immortal golden life he afterward gave her, and the power with him over Anz. And Vekyra must have hated Iru, because of the slave.

"So Vekyra poisoned Iru's wine——"

A paean of joy rose in Price's heart. He drew Aysa aburptly to him, smothered her words with kisses.

"Why are you so glad," she inquired innocently, "that Vekyra poisoned the wine?"

"Never mind, darling. Go on with the story."

"Vekyra herself handed Iru the bowl. The slave-girl was near. She saw the look on Vekyra's face, and cried out, and told Iru not to drink.

"Then Vekyra, to save herself, pretended to be very angry. She cursed the slave-girl. She said she herself would drink the wine, if Iru would give back the girl to her.

"But Iru refused. He was too brave to understand how another could do a cowardly thing. In the haste of his anger, he put the bowl to his own lips. Aysa tried to strike it from his hand; he held her back.

"Aysa then implored the king to let her drink it, rather than he. But he drained the bowl himself. Instantly he fell.

His last breath was a promise that he would return to destroy Vekyra.

"The slave-girl threw herself down upon his body. Vekyra pinned the two together with a dagger she had ready in her clothing, to use if the poison failed. Leaving them so, she escaped from the palace to Malikar, who gave her reward for the thing."

Price did not speak.

The story had removed his last unwilling doubt, the final barrier between them. Now they were one. It seemed to Price as if a vast purpose had come to pass. A unity, an ultimate completeness, emerged from the confused, painful conflict of his life. He knew that every incident in his years of discontented roving had been but a step toward this moment with Aysa in the desert.

The sun descended, reddened. A purple sea, the vast shadow of *Hajar Jehannum* flowed over the rugged basalt plain behind them. Cooler air breathed against their blistered faces; the savage violence of the day surrendered to the mystic peace of twilight.

Aysa moved a little, sighing happily, and relaxed against him. His arm pillowed her fair head. The still desert wrapped them with a peace deeper than Price had ever known, with a quiet happiness that became changeless and enduring as the very desert.

That new peace was not broken when Aysa tensed abruptly in his arms, listening, and asked:

"What is that, humming like a great bee?"

Price heard the distant droning. He pointed out the gray

mote wheeling up against the deepening azure of the south-
ward sky. He knew that it was one of the fighting-planes
that had been called by Jacob Garth's radio.

It came northward, following the trail. Price and Aysa
stood up as it came near; Price took off his shirt and
waved it. The gray ship found them, roared low over
them. Price saw Sam Sorrows, the old Kansan, bareheaded,
leaning recklessly from the cockpit, gesturing with his arms.
He waved in return, and the plane flew back toward the
oasis.

"That is a flying-ship of my own people," he told Aysa.
"We may ride in it back to my land, if you wish. The
man who waved is my friend. The rocks are so rough
that he could not come down here. But he will come for us
tomorrow."

Wide-eyed with wonder, she asked many questions as
the droning of the plane died in purple twilight. Price
answered them, while the ancient stillness of the rock
desert came back and the broad gold disk of the moon
broke above a rugged horizon.

Aysa was eager, excited. But Price's new, joyous peace
lived on in a world of silver light and purple shadow, at
one with silence and mystery that had endured a million
years. She sat by him in the moonlight, and he was content.

GOLDEN BLOOD by Jack Williamson

This first cloth edition of the original text, with revisions, published April 1978, limited to 1500 copies, of which 150 were numbered and signed by the artist and author. Text was set in 12 point Souvenir by Monarch Graphics, San Francisco, California. Separations for dust jacket by Gregory and Falk, San Francisco, California. Technical assistance: Nancy Steele. Text paper is 60# Warrens "1854", an acid-free paper with an extended shelf life. This book was printed and bound by Braun-Brumfield, Ann Arbor, Michigan.